ARCHBISHOP'S CONFESSION

The Father Barrett Files #3

JAMIE MASON

ROUGH
EDGES
PRESS

Archbishop's Confession
Paperback Edition
Copyright © 2022 Jamie Mason

Rough Edges Press
An Imprint of Wolfpack Publishing
5130 S. Fort Apache Rd. 215-380
Las Vegas, NV 89148

roughedgespress.com

Paperback ISBN 978-1-68549-162-8
eBook ISBN 978-1-68549-161-1
LCCN 2022944094

ARCHBISHOP'S
CONFESSION

"Three things cannot be long hidden: the sun, the moon and the truth."

– Buddha

Booze

"...AND ONE LAST THING," said Archbishop Crowe. "We need to talk about your drinking, Father Barrett."

"Yes, your excellency." Barrett took a sip from his wineglass and adjusted the fit of the receiver against his shoulder. He had hoped to end this month's phone call without the subject arising. "What would you like to discuss?"

"When last we met in Campbell River," Crowe continued, "you assured me that you had your alcohol intake under control. But Monsignor Wright tells a different story. Apparently, you've been skipping your scheduled calls with him …?"

"Ah. True." Barrett's transfer to Crowe's archdiocese in Vancouver had been contingent upon an agreement to attend substance abuse counselling. "I've dropped off on the calls. I'll get back on them…"

"Monsignor Wright feels that something more drastic is in order," Crowe interrupted. "And I agree. So we've signed you up with the local chapter of Alcoholics Anonymous."

"Sure. Of course." Barrett let this drop coolly, without the slightest hint of the panic those words inspired. "Pardon me just one sec, your excellency…"

He covered the receiver's mouthpiece, slammed the rest of his wine, and poured another glass. He drank off half before returning to the call.

"Sorry, archbishop. So, AA meetings. Sure thing. Good idea. Are we talking daily or…?"

"There are a series of meetings that run at the community center, sponsored by Reverend Ward of St. Anne's Anglican parish. You're to attend one meeting per week going forward and check in with Reverend Ward."

So, he's got the Anglicans doing his dirty work for him, now, Barrett thought. *Great!*

Aloud, he said: "Of course, your excellency. I shall call Reverend Ward and obtain the schedule so I can—"

"No need. Your first meeting is this afternoon. Two o'clock. You'll meet Reverend Ward there."

"Of course, your excellency."

"Very well. We'll talk again next month. *Dominus vobiscum.*"

Archbishop Crowe hung up, leaving Barrett to fume over his wine.

———

HE LEFT the office and stomped upstairs to the kitchen where the housekeeper Miss Dolan was preparing to leave for the day. She gave him a sidelong glance as he rinsed out his wineglass and put it in the dish drainer.

"A bit early for drinking, isn't it, father?"

"No."

"I see. How was your call with the archbishop?" she asked.

"Oh, fine."

"He's such a wise and compassionate leader is Archbishop Crowe," she said, taking up her purse and car keys. "It must be a tremendous comfort to get to speak with him on a regular basis."

"Oh, yes. *Tremendous…*"

She narrowed her eyes. "I've put a tray in the oven for your dinner, father. Roast beef left over from last night."

I bet she was the one who called Crowe to complain about my drinking, Barrett thought. *She's had it in for me ever since she had to clean up after that dog I had here for a few days…*

"Thank you, Miss Dolan," he said with a smile.

"Good day, father," she sniffed, taking the kitchen garbage out with her as she left.

———

BARRETT HAD NEVER GIVEN his drinking much thought. He just considered it every bit as necessary and part of his daily routine as eating, praying or taking a shower. It was a habit he had picked up soon after joining the City of Toronto police service, where he had worked for six years as a general duty patrolman before becoming a Jesuit. The things he had seen while patrolling Toronto's red zone were haunting – brutal scenes of violence, addiction and neglect that had, like the alcoholism, served as excellent preparation for his work as a priest.

He hadn't spent long in the front lines. After a stint teaching and some time as a parish assistant, the Holy See got wind of his background and assigned him to the Congregation of the Doctrine of the Faith as a Papal investigator. At first, he had liked the job. But successive investigations into sexual and financial misconduct, abuse and neglect had brought him right back to his old days in the red zone. And the drinking had resumed. Along with the violence. Which had led him to this backwater town.

They say God never gives you more than you can handle, and they're right, he thought, walking the quiet sidewalks of Fulton toward the community center. *Because God gave us booze. Praise His Name.*

Two flags, one Canadian and one for the province of BC, hung limply outside the main entrance. Built sometime back in the dim inane of the Seventies, the Fulton Community Center resembled a two-story palette of bricks someone had dumped out and hastily arranged into a public building. No doubt the glass doors and metal fixtures had once appeared futuristic. Now they were as tarnished and tired as the linoleum in the gymnasium Barrett sometimes rented for parish functions. The building existed in a weird sort of historical stasis, as wrung out as a dish towel, as tired as the oldest senior citizen who schlepped in or out of the place.

A glimmer of brightness appeared as Barrett approached the lobby doors and he recognized the shiny chassis of a white RCMP Crown Victoria patrol car. *Gavin must be around here somewhere,* he thought. Gavin Lewis, Fulton's sole full-time police officer, was an RCMP sergeant who had come closest to being something like a friend to Barrett. They kept adjoining stools at the Junction, Fulton's main bar, and had gotten quietly ploughed together on more than one occasion. Gavin Lewis also knew about Barrett's background as a former cop and Papal investigator.

As Barrett watched, an ambulance pulled up behind the Crown Vic and two paramedics emerged, hauling a gurney out of the rear. He hurried over.

"I'm Father Barrett," he said. "What's going on?"

"We have an injury in the fire stairwell," said the male paramedic. Barrett held open the door for him and his female partner, then hurried ahead to run interference for the stretcher team. The blue steel fire door at the rear of the lobby beside the washrooms was being propped open by a facility janitor. Barrett stepped over and relieved him with a smile, holding it wide for the paramedics.

A woman sat on the bottom step of the concrete fire stairs. There was blood on the wall and on the inside of the door. Sergeant Lewis stood by as the woman's bleeding hand was being bandaged by another employee. The bleeding woman half-rose as the paramedics arrived with their stretcher.

"Oh, look. I'm…okay," she said, attempting to laugh. But it was obvious as she tried to stand that she was wobbly on her feet.

"Ginny, just go ahead and sit down." Lewis moved in and placed a friendly hand on her shoulder. "You bumped your head during the incident…"

"Yeah, this is just standard procedure, ma'am." One of the EMTs helped Ginny to the step and knelt before her to examine the wound. "Wow, yeah. That's gonna' need stitches…"

"Gavin, Jesus. What happened?" Barrett leaned toward the Mountie and lowered his voice as the paramedic peeled back bloody bandages to reveal the long, wide cut across the woman's palm.

"She's a janitor here," Lewis replied in a mutter. "Was

doing her rounds when she came across two homeless squatting in here. When she asked them to leave, one pulled a straight razor and..." Lewis glanced to a red smear on the painted cinderblock. Barrett recognized the ridges and whorls of individual fingerprints among the scarlet miasma and felt briefly nauseas.

"Any suspects?" As he often did in Lewis' company, Barrett reverted to his former life as a patrolman.

"Wanted to talk to you about that, actually." Lewis frowned. "You got a few minutes?"

"Sure." Barrett checked his watch. He wasn't due for his AA meeting for another half-hour.

"Come on." Lewis stepped toward the door, turning back to the injured woman on the stairs. "I'm going to catch up with you at the hospital okay, Ginny?"

"I'm fine, Gavin. Fine." She smiled tiredly and Barrett could see disorientation swimming just behind her eyes. *Concussion for sure,* he thought. Ginny would need to be checked out.

Lewis assured her he still needed to take her statement, then led Barrett through the lobby of the community center to his Crown Vic. He waited until they were seated inside, soundproof doors shut, to begin.

"I dunno', padre." Lewis shook his grey head slowly, staring out the window with a kind of weary resignation. "I've been working this town for thirty years, now. But I can't believe the kind of bullshit Walton and I are dealing with on a daily basis nowadays."

"What kind of bullshit?"

"I want to show you something." Lewis put the car in gear and pulled out of the community center lot onto Fulton's main street. The town was still fairly quiet, although pedestrian traffic had picked up in the hour before school let out. They drove past the row of shops in which Lewis and Walton, the Conservation Officer, had their storefront detachment, past boutiques and alleyways and the windowless façade of McLellan's Big Box Retail, Fulton's answer to Walmart. There was a buffer of several streets before the main drag faded into the industrial zone near the highway. Lewis turned up one of these unnamed streets, which rose steadily in a gentle hillock, and pulled onto the shoulder of the road. Visible through the windshield was the section of town through which they had just driven, the community center and big box and rows of shop front stores and offices arrayed in the valley below. "See that mound over there?" Lewis pointed.

Barrett squinted and saw a low hillock that was a combination of grass and sand and discarded items. About a mile from his seat in the cruiser and a few blocks behind the big box, the place didn't really have a name, so was referred to colloquially as 'the Dump.' It was a known hot spot for the indigent, drug users, and high-school beer parties. At the moment, it was a gathering place for a dozen or so homeless with their bags and shopping carts.

"The Dump," Barrett said, rolling down the Crown Vic's window and producing cigarettes. "I've seen it."

Lewis picked a set of field glasses from the glove compartment and handed them over. "Ever seen that skinny guy with the beard before?"

Barrett zeroed in on the man. Tall, thin, with long dark hair and a long beard, he could easily have passed for Jesus with a little grooming except for the sinister vibe he emitted. Something about the way he laughed and held sway with his eyes was more Rasputin than the

Prince of Peace. Barrett, who knew many of Fulton's homeless, had never seen him before.

"Who is he?" He passed back Lewis' binoculars.

"We don't have a name yet. Community center CCTV shows the two assailants running from the building but we have no face shots, nothing distinct we can use to press charges. But witnesses say the two were spotted in this guy's company earlier today." Lewis, the glasses pressed to his eyes, cracked a sour smile. "Know what they're calling him?"

"What?"

"The Garbage Messiah." Lewis lowered the field glasses and sighed. "Padre, you notice the increase in crime, lately? Shoplifting? Mischief and property damage? Assaults like the one at the center?"

Barrett had to admit that things in town had taken a plunge where street crime was concerned in the past months.

"It might be random, but...a lot of it appears to coincide with the arrival of the Messiah in town."

Barrett checked his watch. It was almost time for his AA meeting. "You still planning to meet Ginny at the hospital?"

"Yeah. Walton's already there, taking a statement but I'll join shortly. Meantime, I'm going to keep an eye on the Garbage Messiah. He has kind of a ringleader feel to him. I suspect he's the big fish that might link up some of these unrelated small crimes here in town."

"Makes sense."

"Padre, you willing to help me out on this one?"

Barrett nodded. "Sure, Gavin." It wasn't the first time Lewis had asked Barrett for assistance. "I'll keep my eyes and ears open."

"Thanks." Lewis started the car. "I'll run you back to the center. You have an appointment there, I guess?"

"Yeah. Going to meet the enemy," Barrett sighed. "Someone named Reverend Ward."

"From St. Anne's Anglican?" Lewis smirked. "Oh, the two of you are going to get along just swell..."

Something in Lewis' tone made Barrett uneasy.

Anglicans

LEWIS DROPPED him off at the front door. The woman at the reception desk informed him that the 'Concord Room,' the location for the AA meetings, was on the second floor. So Barrett hoofed it up there, turning bits of the conversation with Lewis over in his mind.

The cop was right, of course. Petty crime had soared in the past few months and violent attacks like the one on Ginny the janitor were becoming more frequent. Barrett wondered about Lewis' hypothesis that the 'Garbage Messiah' was the cause of all this change. It was a clever hypothesis that seemed, upon reflection, a little paranoid. Barrett wondered if perhaps his old friend Lewis might be cracking under the strain of his job.

He's been the sole cop here in Fulton for a long time, he thought, pacing past the rooms in the second-floor hallway, each one identified by a nameplate. He was seeking Concord. It turned out to be the one with the door standing open. He went in.

A circle of chairs occupied the center of the room.

That was all it contained, aside from a woman tacking a poster onto a bulletin board. Barrett stepped in and cleared his throat. The woman turned.

"You must be Father Barrett," she said. Fortyish, lithe and sharp-eyed, she wore jeans and a sleeveless t-shirt. A tangle of silver jewelry hung from her neck, a mismatch of leather thongs and silver chains from which dangled decorative bits, the largest of which was a cross. Barrett took in the blue-tinted hair, bare feet and web of tattoos spiraling up both arms.

"Yeah." He smiled. "I've come to meet with Reverend Ward. Is he here?"

"Reverend Ward *is* here." She smirked, padded over to some sneakers discarded beside a chair, and stuffed her feet into them. "You're speaking to her."

"Ah." Barrett offered a tight smile. "Forgive me. Um…" He stepped over, a hand extended. "I'm Mike."

"Kelly." She seized his hand, pumped it twice, and let go to step back, hands on her hips. "I take it Archbishop Crowe didn't warn you that you'd be dealing with a lady priest."

"No. But, uh…" He fought to loosen the smile's tightness. "That won't be a problem."

"Oh!" She feigned relief. "Well! So glad I merit your approval, father." She spoke in a broadly sarcastic tone, softening the salvo with a smirk.

"I didn't mean it that way…"

"Relax." She waved a hand. "I'm just breaking balls. It's nice to meet you, Mike. For real. And I'm glad you're here. Welcome."

"So glad you acknowledge my balls are there to break," he fired back in a jolly but competitive tone. "Of course, that leaves me at a disadvantage. Since you don't have any of your own…"

"Oh, ho *ho!*" Her eyes narrowed but her grin widened. "Should my testicle deficiency disqualify me from the pulpit, padre? It didn't disqualify me from national service…"

"You ex-Forces?"

"Damn straight. I'm a dirty Princess Pat."

"I'm an ex-cop." Barrett grinned as he took a seat in one of the chairs. The Princess Patricia's Canadian Light Infantry, one of Canada's most recognized and celebrated military regiments, was known for its relentless professionalism and high state of military readiness. *If she was a Princess Pat, then she's a badass,* Barrett thought. A hard-charging attitude was what it took to be part of the regiment that had been handling Canada's "dirty work" for a century and whose motto is *"First in the Field."*

"A cop, hey?" She sat in a nearby chair, folding a leg under her on the seat. "I bet you can identify with this thought. Going from an armed service into the ministry is like… Well, you're still serving society, just with a different tool. The carrot instead of the stick."

"Never heard it put quite that way before." Her words ignited a shock of recognition in his belly. "But it's true. And society requires both."

"Up to a point." She spread her hands. "I mean, you have to admit…We've gone *way* overboard as a society in terms of our devotion to social order. It's led to a regimented, overly-controlled environment that's toxic to children, women, minorities…"

"Oh, here we go!" Barrett uttered a sharp bark of laughter. "You really *believe* that, Kelly? That society is overly controlled? Our schools are war zones! The welfare and healthcare systems are strained to the breaking point. Theft and street crime are skyrocketing. What's your solution?"

"All that stuff is the result of how society is structured."

"It's the result of *sin,* Kelly!" Barrett was surprised to find himself becoming heated. "We can't blame people's failure to take personal responsibility on a society that indulges their every whim and weirdness!"

"A-ha!" She raised a forefinger. "*'A society that indulges their every whim and weirdness.'* Like what, exactly? Trans children? Gay people?" She grinned tauntingly. "Female priests?"

"Now, I didn't say—"

"Hey, I get it! After centuries of privilege, equality must feel like oppression."

"After centuries of *progress,* pulling down society must feel like *accomplishment* to people who never contributed to *building* that society. Who were content to *take* from it, all the while denouncing the framework that guarantees their safety, food, shelter…"

She was grinning widely now, chuckling and shaking her head. Like Barrett, she was encountering someone whose values differed so diametrically from her own that they demanded debate. But at the same time, she relished having an intelligent and articulate opponent.

"You're a sharp one, Mike." She laughed. "Gotta say. Real sharp. So…why the drinking?"

"We can discuss that," he allowed. "But first, I want to know about your discussion with Archbishop Crowe. How did…? I mean, whatever possessed him to…?"

"Go to the enemy?" Her eyes twinkled with mischief. "He likes you, you know. Respects the hell out of you. Doesn't want to lose a man he considers 'a valuable asset to the church.' That's high praise, Mike."

"What about you?" Barrett gazed at the poster she had just tacked up. It listed the Twelve Steps of AA that were widely accepted in the recovery movement. "How did you wind up supervising AA meetings?"

She grew quiet. It was a fascinating change to witness. Barrett enjoyed the woman's commanding personality. But to watch her become reflective showed she had some real bottom to her. He wondered how good she was in the pulpit.

"I went through a stage," she admitted. "Near the end of my time in seminary. It was a real dark period, Mike. I was about to get married when my fiancé... cheated on me. And, well..."

"Jesus. I'm sorry."

"Me, too." She sighed. Barrett saw tears glimmering in her eyes as she looked away. "I hit the sauce, man. Hit it hard. It changed me. I almost flunked out. Fortunately, my advisor noticed and intervened. I got some therapy. Went to some meetings. Pulled out of the nose-dive and managed to get myself ordained. So now, when there's a need, I do this." She gestured to encompass the interior of the Concord Room.

Barrett sat quiet for a long minute. "That's a hell of a story, Kelly. Thank you for telling me."

"You're welcome. He was ex-Princess Pat's, too."

"He was an idiot."

"Ha. You're not wrong." She looked back at him with real affection. "And what about you, Mike? Good-looking guy. Macho. Ex-cop. Why aren't you married to some warm, lovely woman and living with her in the suburbs behind some nice white picket fence?"

"Warm and lovely haven't exactly been in plentiful supply in my life." He shrugged. "Bad childhood. Dysfunctional socialization. A whole lot of bad breaks..." He shrugged again. "I'm not husband material. Or even friend material. Really."

Voices rose in the corridor outside. Others were gathering for the meeting.

"How was your childhood dysfunctional?" she asked softly.

"My dad was in the mob. I saw him shoot a guy when I was six."

She absorbed this in watchful silence.

"We're about to get started here," she said quickly. "What are you doing later tonight?"

————

IT WAS ONLY as he was walking home that it hit him.

Wait. Did I just agree to go out on a date?

He shook his head. No, that sort of thing wasn't possible! But he realized he should be more careful. Certainly, he had agreed to meet up with Reverend Ward later for coffee. But he couldn't assume that just because he viewed her as another member of the clergy that others would view their association in an innocent light. Barrett recalled the negative image of the church under which he had labored as an investigator for the Holy See. Of course, most priests aren't perverts. But try convincing the average man in the street of that after the onslaught of salacious media publicity about pedophile priests. Where clergy are concerned, people automatically assume wrongdoing where matters of sexual discretion are concerned.

He resolved not to allow the image of the church to suffer. His posting here was, after all, probationary. Should he cause further scandal, he would no doubt be sent to some garden spot like Iraq or rural Nepal.

And good luck getting ahold of booze if it's in the former!

Alright, then. He would have to remain sober for the next few hours. He would shower and shave. Maybe take a nap. Put on a fresh set of clerical vestments…

Relax, he told himself. *You're not going out on a date…*

Was he?

He returned home and let himself in. Miss Dolan was, blessedly, gone. The dog with which he'd been saddled for a time following the departure of an elderly parishioner into long-term care was also (blessedly) gone. The house was dark and quiet in the cool, cloudy afternoon. Ordinarily, the perfect time for a drink. But he would hold off, in the spirit of his new…

Sponsor? Friend? Whatever the hell she is?

Perhaps that was the logic behind Archbishop Crowe's choice to place Barrett into a program. Kelly Ward was ideally suited to be his AA sponsor, even if she was (in truth) an amateur where alcoholism was concerned.

A bad bout of blackout drinking during your last year in seminary? He sniffed. *Try spending a decade or two like that and see if you have what it takes to turn pro.*

Still. She was frank and sincere…

Feminist weirdo…

Compassionate and articulate…

Hippie!

Eager to serve her community…

Probably a communist!

Nevertheless, he was smiling thoughtfully as he made his way downstairs to the basement office.

He dropped into his office chair and switched on the computer. There, glowing on the screen, was the same blank Microsoft Word page with the blinking cursor that had been taunting him all week. Next Sunday's sermon still eluded him, and the scheduled Bible reading did nothing for him. He was tempted to venture elsewhere in Scripture for inspiration and so summoned up a web browser and went to his favorite Biblical reference portal. He typed in the word 'wine' and was rewarded.

> Let him kiss me with the kisses of his
> mouth—
> For your love is more delightful than
> wine...
> Take me away with you—let us hurry!
> Let the king bring me into his chambers.

He thought of silver jewelry, of bare feet and tattoos spiraling up sleeveless arms...

Stop it!

His computer beeped. This threw him at first, until he remembered that Father Dolan, his housekeeper's brother-in-law and interim priest, had installed some damned, newfangled videoconferencing application with the bad habit of interrupting him when he was trying to think. A mini screen appeared, asking if he would accept a call from Archbishop Crowe.

Crowe again? Barrett sighed, clicked YES and waited.

Deacon Blues

"FATHER BARRETT!" Archbishop Crowe (or, more accurately, his bust) beamed at Barrett from a window on the computer screen. "I saw you were online so hazarded a call."

He saw I was online? Barrett panicked. Did that mean Crowe knew when he was using the computer? That seemed unbelievable. Almost…*Stalinesque*. Barrett gritted his teeth. *Is this what the world has come to?* Ridiculous! He decided to start composing his sermons on the typewriter. He reasoned through all this within a few seconds of Crowe's sudden appearance on his desktop, then pasted a wan smile on his face.

"Your excellency, hello! What a…surprise. Here I was working on my sermon for next Sunday and, well…Ta-da! Pop goes the archbishop. So to speak."

Crowe responded with a dry chuckle. "What text will you base your homily upon?"

"Ah, Song of Songs."

"Well, be sure to avoid the smutty stuff," Crowe said lightly. "Wouldn't want to inspire flights of lustful fancy in our parishioners, would we? Anyway, I'm glad I caught you, Mike. There's something important we need to discuss."

"Certainly, your excellency. At your service. What can I do for you?"

"You have developed a rather good working relationship with the local tribe, haven't you." It wasn't a question. "That's no easy thing. You'll recall I served at that parish as a young ordained. The tribe kept me at arm's length throughout my tenure. But apparently, you've somehow managed to win over the Chief."

"I have?" Barrett was confused. His interactions with the tribe had been awkward to say the least. He had been assaulted by a gang of First Nations youth soon after his arrival and gotten into a fistfight with one shortly after. The Chief had bailed him out of jail and declined to press charges, but Barrett had intervened during a riot some time later when the Chief and his people had attempted to burn down a local housing development. Barrett had skated through all of these episodes by the skin of his teeth. If the Chief was impressed, it was news to him.

"Yes. That's what I'm told. By Danny."

"Danny?"

"Danny Robert. A newly ordained priest. Took his vows two months ago. He's native to that tribe. And I'm about to place him with you as your new deacon."

Barrett digested this piece of news silently.

"He's a very capable young man. In fact, Father Barrett, you will find he is willing and eager to help lighten a parish priest's load with real conscience and a servant heart. I offer him…" Crowe chuckled. "I offer Danny Robert by way of a bribe, actually."

"Bribe?" Barrett actually laughed. "I am your excellency's willing servant. I know I'm…difficult. But I am a sworn man of the cloth. Whatever my archbishop needs…"

"Mike, relax. And when we talk privately, please call me Andrew."

"I. Uh. What? *Andrew?* Andrew. Okay. Andrew."

"That's better." Crowe smiled. "I am going to need your assistance in a very delicate matter here in the next few days. Something involving historical business at the parish that must be handled with extreme discretion."

"Of course, your—uh, Andrew."

"Good." Crowe looked down and fiddled with something on his desktop. "What I'd like to do is bring Danny Robert into our video conference now and introduce you."

"Fine. Fine!"

Another sound—a sort of blaring beep—arose and the window framing Crowe's face split and a second bust appeared. The face that peered out was that of a young man in his mid-twenties. Dark skinned with black hair and brown eyes, he bore all the classic features of west coast First Nations people. His smile was shy and Barrett could tell he had a humble manner about him. But it could not hide the intelligence glimmering in his eyes.

"Father Barrett, hello. I'm Danny Robert."

"Hi, Danny. Mike Barrett. Nice to meet you. I hear you're going to come and help me take care of St. Michael's and St. Joan's."

"With your and Archbishop Crowe's permission, I hope to."

"Ah, father?" Crowe interrupted. "There will be a slight change to ordinary procedure where your new deacon is concerned. Because his family lives on the nearby reserve, he won't be staying with you in the parsonage but rooming at home with his family."

"That sounds fine," Barrett said, managing to hide the great relief this news inspired.

———

HE FINALLY MANAGED to make some headway on the sermon. He chose as his theme the enchantment of newly found love. For some reason, the topic inspired him. He managed to write two pages of pretty decent stuff.

He decided it was time for a glass to brace himself for his forthcoming visit. He would drink some wine, then brush his teeth and hit the mouthwash. He wanted to be loose but not too loose when he sat down with Kelly Ward for his obligatory sponsoring session.

God, I hope she's not one of these out-of-control evangelists when it comes to substance use and abuse, he thought. That was the last thing he needed just now. In between everything else.

He had just poured himself some wine when his cell-phone buzzed. He looked. There was a text from Kelly.

How many Freudians does it take to screw in a lightbulb?

Barrett chuckled and typed:

I don't know. How many?

A moment later she replied:

Two. One to screw in the bulb and the other to hold my penis. I mean my mother. I mean the ladder.

That made him laugh out loud. He was still laughing when she sent another text.

Screw coffee. How about a drink?

His eyebrows shot upward. He typed:

Your place or mine?

She typed back:

My place. I have a nice Bordeaux. We can sit at the kitchen table, listen to CBC Radio and get gently smashed together while deciding what to tell Archbishop Crowe next time he calls.

Barrett grinned.

I'll be right over.

Over Drinks

HER CHURCH IS WAY NICER *than mine*...

The structure itself was an A-frame design, similar to that of his own church, but larger and more spread out. The tip of the 'A' was the bell tower while the lower portion melted into a one-story rambling, ranch-style main floor of cedar sheathed in steel and glass. The parking lot, similar in design to a traffic circle with ultra-modern signage, was designed to maximize efficient traffic flow. But it was empty now and the building itself dark. As dusk fell, a single light switched on by the door marked 'PARISH OFFICE.' It opened and Barrett swerved in that direction.

"Hello." She stood there, shading her eyes with one hand, the other on the knob. In her bare feet, jeans and sleeveless shirt, she looked more like some biker's girl-friend than a parish priest. When Barrett approached, she moved forward and gave him a hug.

"Hey, thanks," he said, hugging her back. "It's nice to see you again."

"Nice to see you, too, Don Camillo."

He laughed. "Don *Camillo?*" He stepped inside and stood at the head of a flight of steps heading down. "I thought I was the only guy who remembered those stories." Barrett chuckled, remembering the absurdist tales of Italian cartoonist Giovanni Guareschi, about the pugnacious, mystical, anti-communist priest Don Camillo.

"Are you kidding? Don Camillo rocks." Kelly clapped his shoulder and stepped past him. "Come on down. My place is in the basement."

"Oh, I see. Anglicans are economizing by making their priests live in the cellar?"

"Ha. Wait until you see my pad."

She wasn't kidding. When she opened the nonde-script door at the bottom of the steps, Barrett stepped through into an ultra-modern condominium-style living space. Burnished stone flooring alternated with shag carpeting through a series of rooms that more or less hived off of a central living area. Kelly guided him through the laundry cubby with its SpaceX-style washer and dryer modules to the kitchen, which was adorned with retro cabinets and pump-handle style faucet. The living room came equipped with a sunken conversation pit and a flagstone fireplace. An open bottle of wine and two glasses sat waiting on the glass coffee table. Kelly smirked as she took a seat and poured one for him.

"This was unexpected." Barrett sat across from her, kicked off his shoes and shrugged out of his jacket. "I figured we were going to do the usual AA thing and have coffee."

Kelly said nothing. She merely handed him his drink, poured herself one and then raised it in a toast.

"To new friendships," she said quietly.

"I'll drink to that." Barrett touched his glass to hers

and took a tentative sip of hooch. It went down smooth as liquid silk. "Hey, nice vintage!"

"Well, I figure if we're going to explicitly betray the terms of our, ah, *arrangement* with Archbishop Crowe, we might as well do it in style."

"I suppose." She grinned at his discarded jacket and stocking feet. "I see you've made yourself comfortable!"

"Says the chick not wearing any shoes…"

"I haven't been called a 'chick' since high school."

"And I haven't been hugged since then, so I guess we're even."

She grew quiet but he could sense discomfort rippling just below the surface. She looked down, the way some women do when facing unpleasant truths. But when she looked up at him again, her eyes were blazing intently.

"It can't be that simple," she whispered fiercely.

"What can't be?"

"You." She sounded slightly annoyed as she waved a hand. "Haven't been hugged since high school?"

"Not the way you hugged me."

"And how did I hug you, Mike?"

"Like it mattered." He swallowed. It was his turn to look down. "Like what you held in your arms was precious."

She was watching him intently.

"My last three years of high school were more or less spent looking after my mother. She was very ill." Barrett toyed with his wineglass. "I was either caring for her or going to school or working with my dad."

"Dad the mobster?"

"Yeah."

"I'm guessing he wasn't much into hugs." Kelly slid closer to him on the couch and took his hand. It clearly wasn't intended as anything more than a gesture of comfort. She squeezed his fingers. "Go on. Your mom was sick."

"Yeah." Barrett folded his hand around hers, surprised at the comfort her touch afforded. "Yeah, she had degenerative cancer. It was…nasty. It took its time killing her. And the process of caring for her basically sucked away my life between the ages of fifteen and eighteen. Dad, of course, was no help whatsoever. At first, my friends understood and were supportive. But, after a while…"

He sighed and stared at the flames in the fireplace, his stare glassy as it slid into the past.

"After a while they stopped keeping in touch. Stopped calling or stopping by. It didn't happen all at once. It's not like they ostracized me or anything like that. They were teenagers, you know? And life was happening for them. Moving fast. They just…forgot about me."

He closed his eyes and clenched his jaw. He had forgotten how much that had hurt.

"You know what the funny thing is about those years, Kelly? I don't remember any of the days. Only the nights and evenings. That whole section of my life was just like one long, slow autumn dusk. After she died, well… Everyone else was looking forward to senior prom and making college plans. I was breaking down her hospital bed and selling off used equipment to medical supply stores. I remember the first day of summer after graduation. Standing there on the lawn. It was like life was about to start over again after a brief interruption. Except this time I was all alone."

He fought back tears. And failed. He didn't bawl. He merely sat perfectly still, tears cascading from his eyes down his cheeks. He felt Kelly watching him as he continued.

"I found out that my old group of friends were… getting together. Sort of a farewell dinner. They were all going their separate ways—to jobs, university, out of the city, what-have-you… We'd all been friends since elementary school. I didn't find out because I was invited. No, I heard it through a third party. *Over*heard it, actually. I hadn't hung out with the bunch of them for a while but remained on good terms with each individually. When I ran into one, I mentioned it would be nice to get together again. That my mother had passed on so now I had the time. I mentioned how much I'd missed everybody."

"And what did he say?"

"He, um, made some vague excuses. Didn't mention the get-together." Barrett shrugged. "It was due to happen the next night. At a local restaurant—a little Italian place that we all knew. It had been around forever. I thought perhaps I'd go down and surprise them. Just show up. What would they do?"

"So you thought, *Fuck them, I'll just go.* Like that?"

"No, I…" His breath fixed on a knot of frustration. "I wasn't even thinking like that. Not at first, anyway. I honestly thought they'd be glad to see me, you know? That they felt the same way about me as I felt about all of them." He blinked hard. "I wanted them to know how I felt about them. How important they were to me. And I wanted to thank them."

"So." She squeezed his hand again. "What happened?"

"May I smoke?"

"Sure." She smiled. "Go ahead."

Barrett fumbled out his cigarettes, offered her one,

was surprised when she accepted. He lit both before continuing the story.

"So, I knew where and when the dinner was taking place. The restaurant was called Luigi's and it was within walking distance of everyone's home. We'd been meeting there on and off for years. I waited until a half-hour after the party started before heading out. I walked through the dark streets by myself, a little keyed up and a little uneasy…I honestly wasn't sure how I'd be greeted. But then I was crossing the parking lot toward the place. It had a big glass wall around the dining room so I could see the table with my friends. I stopped to take in the sight of them.

"They were in there, laughing and toasting each other with glasses of wine. At first, I was…*delighted.*" He smiled, remembering. "My *friends.* Looking so happy and confident and grown-up. I was proud of them. And I wanted them to know that. But as I watched, I realized something else.

"I realized that they were my friends. But I wasn't theirs. Not anymore. For them, time had moved on without me. I was somebody *from the past.* They were friends *in the here and now.* It's difficult to say how I came to see or understand that. But it grew clearer with each passing second that I stood there watching from the shadows of the parking lot. I must have stayed for, like, ten or fifteen minutes maybe. And I remembered that I had not been invited. That it might actually be *rude* to go and crash the party. They probably wouldn't kick me out. But I'd be left with the knowledge that I had put the damper on their fun. Because it was *theirs.* Not mine. Not now. Not anymore."

"So, what did you do?" She moved to the fireplace to

flick ashes, then brought down a little clay ashtray from the mantel and set it before Barrett.

"Thanks." He tapped his cigarette. "I went home. It was a Friday night and my father was out of town on business. Wouldn't be back until the middle of the next week. That was the first time I ever got drunk. That night. My parents kept a wine cellar. I went down and got myself a bottle. Drank the whole thing by myself sitting at the dining room table in the dark. I was sick as a dog the next morning. But…"

He paused.

His wineglass sat before him, half-full. He hadn't taken a drink in something like fifteen minutes. And, strangely, he didn't feel like having one all of a sudden.

"Hungry?" She nudged him.

"What? Yeah. Actually, yeah. I am."

"C'mon." She stubbed out her cigarette and stood. "I have corn chips in the kitchen. Help me make some guacamole."

"Sure!" His own enthusiasm surprised him. He was suddenly ravenous.

Back in the retro country kitchen, Kelly fished two avocados out of the fridge. "Grab that cutting board would you, Mike? I'm putting you to work on chopping detail. Here." She laid an onion and two tomatoes on the board before him. Barrett fished a knife from the butcher block and got to work. It didn't take them long to whip up a bowl of well-seasoned guacamole. They ate it with corn chips, standing at the counter.

"So, when do I get to hear your life story?" he asked.

"Why any time you like, father." She batted her eyelashes demurely. "I'll have to fill you in on my teenage adventures, including my brilliant martial arts career."

"Martial arts?" He raised his eyebrows. "Really?"

"Yes, indeed."

"You the karate kid?" he joked.

"Um, judo. Actually." She feigned a shallow curtsey. "I was a provincial medalist my junior year."

"Cool. You should start a club in your parish."

"I've thought about it." She shrugged. "We have a few kids who might be interested. Otherwise, I don't know who we'd invite."

"Maybe some kids from my church. And I'd come." Barrett held up a hand. "I'm no provincial champ, but judo was a major component of our self-defense program in Toronto police service."

"Oh, *yeah?*" A mischievous twinkle lit her eye. "Think you could take me, padre?"

"Well, I didn't—"

She pounced.

Caught him completely by surprise. *What?* But soon his cop instincts kicked back in and he dealt with her playful attack as he would any incident on the street: by creating distance, bringing hands up, studying his opponent's movements.

She was fast and fluid. But also soft. It gave her movements some subtlety. She grasped his wrist, turned into him and brought him over her hip, loaded up for a throw.

"How're your breakfalls?" she asked.

"Go ahead," he panted.

She launched him over her hip, Barrett tucked his chin, rolled and slapped the carpet to absorb the shock of the fall as he had been taught to do in police training. She reached out and helped him up.

"You're pretty good, Kelly," he said. And meant it.

"Thanks." She hugged him. "I'm glad I met you, Mike. I really am."

Night Rhythms

HE WAS WEARING *a white suit and a straw boater. In his hands was a long pole used to propel the boat by pushing off the river bottom. Sunlight danced on the water…*

With a jangle of bells.

…and Kelly Ward was there, up on the prow, wearing a white lace sundress and trailing her hand in the water, turning from time to time to laugh…

Like a jangle of bells.

…and he would laugh with her. To either side of the river, lush pastures dotted with grazing cows rolling into the distance…

With a jangle of bells. And another one.

Barrett opened his eyes and groaned. The phone on his bedside table was ringing. He rubbed his face, sat up and switched on the lamp before answering.

"Hello? Father Barrett here." He squinted at the clock. It was 2:30 AM.

"Padre?" It was Gavin Lewis. "Sorry to wake you. But I figured you'd want to know. Walton and I have rolled up on your church. Looks like we might have a break-in."

He was already swinging out of bed. "I'll be right over," he growled and hung up.

Once again, he had fallen asleep fully clothed but that was all to the good right now. Pushing his feet into shoes, he rose and grabbed for his blazer. As he hurried through the kitchen toward the back door, he pulled open the drawer by the fridge and stared down at the matte black Glock 19 emblazoned with the Papal arms that he'd carried as a Vatican investigator. He thought of Ginny the janitor and her bleeding hand, of the increased violence and property crimes in town and was tempted to snatch it out and jam it into his belt.

Not here, he reminded himself. *You're not authorized to carry as a municipal peace officer...*

But the trouble was at his church.

Catholic territory.

He grabbed up the pistol, stuffed it into his waist-band and sprinted for the church

———

IT WAS a short distance from the rectory—a five-minute, unhurried walk. Barrett sprinted and made it there in two. Lewis' Crown Vic and Walton's Conservation Service truck were parked just up the block, lights out. Barrett went to the window of the Crown Vic and crouched. Walton and Lewis were watching the church from the front seat. Lewis rolled down the window.

"What have we got?" Barrett asked.

"Watch," whispered Lewis.

Barrett fixed his eyes on the building. An earlier A-frame design than Kelly's, the parish of St. Michael's and

St. Joan's featured a great glass front wall, allowing people in the street to look right into the sanctuary as they passed by. Barrett saw globes of light wink on and off inside. *Flashlights.*

"Son-of-a-bitch," he whispered. "Someone's robbing my church!"

"Don't worry, padre," said Lewis. "We'll get 'em. Adam? You ready?"

"Sure am, Gavin." The conservation officer caressed the pump-action shotgun he held in his lap. "Loaded up with rock salt."

"Okay. You head around back. The padre and I will go in the front door."

"Sounds good."

Walton rolled out of the passenger door and kept to the shadows at the edge of the property as he moved quickly, crouched low. Lewis slipped out of the driver's side door and led the way up the path to the church door, an unlit flashlight in his left hand, his right curled around the butt of his holstered Sig Sauer.

"We'll give Walton a moment or two to get posted," Lewis whispered. "Padre, why don't you get your keys and get set for a quick entrance?"

"Will do." Barrett fished out his key ring. By feel, he located the key with the big square head that opened the main entrance. He positioned himself to one side of the door. Lewis took the other. As quietly as he could, Barrett slid the key into the lock and turned. Then he eased open the door an inch or two and stood back.

Lewis kicked it open and switched on the flashlight, its beam lashing into the dark. Barrett saw movement in the church: figures in black vaulting pews, ducking, scattering. One dropped something as he dashed toward the rear. Barrett recognized his good silver communion chalice. *Bastards!* He reached for his gun.

"Freeze and put your hands up!" Lewis barked.

Barrett heard smashing glass, then a yell. Then the lights came on in the sanctuary and Walton appeared near the altar, shotgun held at port arms as he looked around for the source of the shout. Barrett and Lewis came charging down the center aisle toward him.

"I saw them come this way!" cried Walton. "But I lost 'em!"

"Offices!" Barrett cried, pointing. "To the left!"

Behind the altar was a short hallway leading to the vestry and church offices. Barrett plunged into the shadows. The door to the vestry was open and he could hear voices. But rounding the corner, he saw an empty room. It took him a moment to spot the broken glass on the floor.

Someone shrieked outside. They heard crashing foliage followed by the sound of running footsteps.

"You stay put, padre," ordered Lewis. "Adam and I will go."

They left the room at double-time. Once Barrett heard the big church door fall shut behind them, he drew the Glock and went to the window. He switched on the flashlight app of his cellphone. Then he raised the Glock, steadied it on the wrist of the hand holding the cellphone and peered through the mouth of broken glass with its jagged teeth.

The foliage was still trembling from the intruders' passage. Barrett swept the lights back and forth, searching for some sign of them but saw nothing. He only heard the distant voices of Lewis and Walton searching the underbrush.

"Hhhh…"

He looked down.

She lay tangled in the ferns at the base of the wall. All of nineteen, she had a pretty face—that portion of it visible within the raised folds of her black hoodie. She wore black pants and dark hiking boots and her hands were folded over her abdomen. Turning her face toward Barrett's light, she opened her lips to speak. A trickle of blood ran out from between her clenched teeth and down her chin. She inhaled and tried to speak again.

"Hhhh…"

Barrett glanced down and noticed the blood seeping from between her fingers.

He sprinted into the church office, grabbed the First Aid kit, and ran outside as quickly as he could. Scanning with the cellphone's flashlight, he followed the wall outside through the bushes to the broken vestry room window. She was struggling to breathe when he got there.

"Okay, okay…" He placed the First Aid kit on the ground and knelt beside it. "Let me…" She started and twisted away when he reached for her but there was nowhere to go—only into the wall of the church. Barrett held up a hand.

"Sweetheart," he said, "relax. I'm not mad at you and I'm not going to hurt you. But you've been injured."

"Cut!" she hissed. *"He cut me!"*

"Lift up your hands. *Thaaat's* it. Good." He tugged aside the folds of her hoodie. "Now tell me who cut you."

"He did." And then suddenly she was laughing, a touch hysterically as she enunciated her laughter in hard barks, shaking her body and causing fresh blood to gout from the groove in her stomach. When she coughed, a patch of blood bubbled to her lips. Barrett grabbed two

square bandages and began stuffing them into the wound, trying not to think about the squishing sound they made whenever they moved.

Christ, she's lost a lot of blood, he thought.

Lewis crashed through the bushes, stopped, and whistled. "Holy shit, padre!"

"Call an ambulance, Gavin. She's lost a ton of blood and is going into shock."

"Right." Lewis bushwhacked back toward his Crown Victoria. Barrett heard the mutter of his discussion with island dispatch. Then, in the distance, the plaintive wail of an approaching ambulance.

————

"WHO KNIFED HER?"

"She said, '*He* did.'" Barrett shook his head, swished the last of his vending machine coffee around in the bottom of its cardboard cup, and looked around the hospital waiting room. "And she said the pronoun with distinct reverence. She doesn't particularly strike me as the church-going type."

"She said *he*?" Lewis stood at the picture window at the hospital parking lot as dawn broke in the distance. "Like that's supposed to mean something?"

"To her, it obviously did. The thing is…" Barrett struggled to formulate his statement. "The way she said it sort of suggested…it was somehow okay that he'd stabbed her. That it was almost…I dunno'. Like some kind of blessing or sacrament or something. *HE did!* Like the way you might say your favorite movie star signed his autograph for you."

Gavin considered all of this, head down, hands on his

hips. He stood that way for a long time—long enough that Barrett began to worry, remembering his concern that the old lawman might be strained to the breaking point. When Walton entered the waiting room and Lewis looked up, his weathered face looked haunted and gaunt.

"I spoke to her, Gavin." The conservation officer was putting away his notebook and pen. "She woke up for ten minutes. Was pretty lucid. I asked if she wanted to press charges."

"What did she say?"

"She said, '*Not against him. Never against him.*'"

Lewis swore a blue streak of the filthiest language Barrett had ever heard. The rage boiling up in his voice was terrible—almost frightening in its intensity. When he turned his face to Walton, it was ablaze.

"Adam," he said softly. "I'm going to ask you to stay with her a while, okay? Just give it another hour to see if she comes around again. If she does, ask her *again*. Okay?"

Walton nodded, plainly unsettled.

"Padre, could you come with me?" Lewis stalked toward the door and out into the parking lot. Barrett followed. Lewis said nothing as they got into his Crown Victoria and pulled out of the lot. Lewis guided the police car away from Fulton District Hospital in the direction of town. A few blocks from main street, he pulled over on the rise that overlooked the Dump. He switched off the car and they sat glaring down at the fire burning in the homeless camp there.

"Forgive me, father," Lewis said quietly.

Mastering his surprise, Barrett asked, "Do you want to make a confession, Gavin?"

"I want you to pray for me, father." Lewis hands,

fisted around the steering wheel, were trembling. "And I'm serious."

"Gavin…of course…"

"I've *never* wanted to kill a man this badly before!"

"Murder is a cardinal sin."

"I think the bigger sin may be allowing that man to live. Why does God keep doing this to us, Mike? Why does He keep putting us in these no-win situations, forced to choose the lesser of two evils?"

"We're not supposed to choose evil at all."

"We're supposed to let the innocent suffer?"

"No, Gavin." Barrett reached out and put a hand on Lewis' arm. "We're supposed to help the innocent and the suffering and leave punishment of the guilty to God. Vengeance is His."

"I've never been a God man," Lewis said woodenly. "But I've got a God-sized appetite for vengeance, myself." He sighed. "Pray for me, Mike."

Deacon News

HE HAD Lewis drop him off at the church, where he conducted a quick inventory. Last week's collection money had been stolen, along with some silver candlesticks and every box of matches in the place. Barrett put in a call to a local contractor and made an appointment to get the vestry window fixed. Then he poked around in the maintenance closet until finding a hammer, nails and a sheet of plywood big enough to cover the broken pane. After hammering this into place, he set the alarm, locked the door, and returned home. Miss Dolan was tidying up the kitchen when Barrett stumbled through, looking like something the cat dragged in.

"Another rough night, eh, father?" She smirked down at the dishes she was washing in the sink.

"The church got broken into last night." Barrett stretched. "A young woman was knifed and left to bleed to death outside. I'm just back from the hospital now."

"My goodness! The church? Broken into?" Her outrage at this manifested in more vigorous scrubbing of a pan. "Whatever is this world coming to, father?"

"Beats me." He sighed. "Listen, I'm going upstairs to grab a few hours' sleep. If anyone calls or comes by, could you take a message? I need to rest."

"Certainly, father." Miss Dolan's normally severe facial expression softened to one of concern. "It would not do to have the shepherd of our flock exhausted. You must remain fit and alert to fight off the wolves."

"Quite so. Thanks."

Barrett went into his room and lay down, troubled by her Biblical allusion. He drained off the half-glass of wine he'd left on the bedside table, then fell asleep.

He dreamed of wolves.

———

SHE WAS GONE when he awoke. He showered, changed and then sat down to consume the breakfast she'd made and saved for him. He contemplated the coffee pot for a full minute before rising and pouring himself a glass of wine to go with his bacon and eggs. (It was, after all, a little after 10 AM…) He was just taking his first sip when the phone rang.

"Hello?"

"Father Barrett, hi. It's Danny Robert, your new deacon."

"Danny, hello." Barrett smiled. "Good to hear from you. I expect you'll be coming by sometime soon?"

"I'll be going to the church first," he said, sounding almost apologetic. "I ran into your housekeeper shopping at McLellan's and she told me about the break-in. So I spoke to the contractor. I've arranged to be there at the church when he arrives to repair the window. Archbishop Crowe gave me a set of keys."

"That's great!" Barrett heaved a sigh of relief. The kid

hadn't even showed up for his first day of work and was already making a contribution. "I really appreciate that, Danny. I was up into the wee hours this morning dealing with the break-in. I'm beat. And I still have to touch base with RCMP about it."

"Of course, father. We can get together at your convenience. In the meantime, is there anything I can do to help you prepare for the next church service?"

The kid's a Godsend, Barrett thought. "As a matter of fact, yes," he said. "You'll find printouts of the bulletin for next week's service on my desk. Can you bring them to the print shop? They'll have a box with this week's bulletins ready for pick-up…"

"I'll grab it, father. No problem. Also…I think the church could do with a dusting and vacuuming. Those thieves left a mess behind."

"Oh, Danny. You're awesome." Barrett felt as if a great weight were being lifted from his shoulders. He began to understand what Archbishop Crowe had meant by offering Danny as a bribe. "We can all learn from your example, kid. Seriously. Being of help to one's mentors is a great thing."

Danny laughed. "Well, I learned from Archbishop Crowe. Did you know he used to be the parish priest at this church?"

"I did." Barrett remembered that Danny Robert was from the local tribe and so had some historical knowledge of the parish. "Do you remember those days?"

"Not really. It was before my time. But my grandmother and sister remember," Danny said. "They talk about how Father Crowe, as he was known back then, was a great help to the Archbishop at the time. A man named Radcliffe."

"Radcliffe." The name rang a faint bell for Barrett. "I

seem to recall hearing about him before. Retired now, isn't he?"

"He would be. Yes, father." Danny paused. "Honestly, I don't know what the details were. But there was some sort of scandal. This was back in the day. From the time before he was Archbishop. Perhaps when he was a bishop, or even a priest."

"Go on…" Barrett was fascinated.

"Well, I don't really know much." Danny chuckled. "But my grandmother stopped going to church because of him. She'd never say why. There used to be a lot more Indian people at this parish. Whenever the subject comes up, the elders get really, really quiet."

"Is that right?" Barrett ran a finger around the rim of his wineglass. "And Archbi-…I mean, *Father* Crowe?"

"He's the only one the elders ever mention," said Danny. "They say he's a good man."

Barrett smiled. "I think he is, Danny."

"I think so, too. I'll take care of those things and then wait to hear from you, father."

"Sounds good. Thanks for calling, Danny."

———

"OUR GIRL IS STILL unconscious up at the hospital." Gavin Lewis poured Barrett a cup of coffee, then replaced the decanter in the percolator and resumed a seat behind his desk. "But we did…let's see here…" He sorted through a mountain of file folders. "Ah! Got it. We did get an ID on her." He flipped open a folder. "Sarah Jackson. That's her name. Local island girl. Comes from Oak Bay."

"So, she's a rich kid?" Barrett recognized the name of

Victoria's swankiest neighborhood. He took a cautious sip of Lewis' legendarily bad coffee.

"That's a fair assumption, given that you're going to pay two million for a starter home in that neck of the woods." He scanned the file. "Our Sarah disappeared from Oak Bay two months ago. Saanich police put out a BOLO alert. Near as we can tell, she got to Fulton a few weeks ago. Walton thinks he's seen her around, though he can't remember where." He frowned. "She familiar to you at all, padre?"

Barrett shook his head.

"Can't say I've seen her around, either." Lewis closed the file and switched on his computer. "Adam and I have been talking. We've decided we're going to change up the patrol schedule." He tilted the monitor so Barrett could see the screen. "We're going to go for a twenty-four-hour coverage schedule. Haven't had to do that for a few years but I think it's a good idea. Given the rise in petty crime. And now this."

Barrett examined the spreadsheet. Since his arrival in town, Lewis and Walton had worked tandem and overlapping shifts. Both carried cellphones for after-hours emergencies but most of the police business in town was relatively straightforward and could be handled during the regular workday. Lewis had now changed it up so he would be patrolling town by day and Walton by night.

"That's a punishing schedule," Barrett commented.

"Yeah." Lewis sighed and pushed back from the desk, putting his hands behind his head and stretching. "That's where I was hoping you could help, Mike. Would you consider maybe taking an afternoon patrol for us? Maybe once every eight days just so we can get some rest?"

"Sure." Barrett shrugged. Lewis had taken advantage of his background as a cop before to request help on investigations. Hopping into the car and taking a turn about town was no hardship at all. "Have you reached out to the detachment in Campbell River?"

"I have. They'll see what they can do to offer relief. But they're stretched thin, too. Similar issues. Mostly the homeless. Petty crime."

"Things are tough all over." Barrett changed the subject. "Gavin, you've been here a long time. Almost thirty years, yeah?"

"Give or take." Lewis sipped his coffee. "Why?"

"What do you know about a man named Radcliffe? He's a retired archbishop who apparently has some connection to the town. My new deacon mentioned him."

"Deacon…" Lewis squinted. "That's like an rookie priest, isn't it?"

"It's a post that's often given to newly-ordained priests, yeah," Barrett explained. "This guy I've got is great. Local guy. Name of Danny Robert."

"Danny Robert?" Lewis grinned. "Danny, I remember him. Bit of a hell raiser when he was younger. Got some kind of scholarship and moved away, I seem to recall."

"He ended up in seminary."

"Well, good for him! I imagine having priests that are First Nations is helpful to the Catholic Church."

"Absolutely. It's especially important for our work here in Canada." Barrett paused, considering. "Gavin, were you here when Andrew Crowe was pastor at my church?"

"Oh. That was a *long* time ago." Lewis considered. "Let's see. I got here during the Clinton years. Didn't have much contact with your church back then, honestly. But, now that you mention it." He drummed his fingers on the desk. "Danny Robert...Danny Robert... He's Louise Joe's grandson, isn't he?"

"I don't know, to be honest."

"Fairly sure he is. I think I recall seeing her at a few softball games." Lewis had the bit in his teeth now. Leaning forward in his chair, elbows on the desk, he searched his memory. "Old Louise Joe used to be married to a man named Gordon. Gordon Joe. He's long dead. But when he was alive, *man.* Just about the biggest badass you'd ever want to meet. Dangerous. Man had a temper like... Well, there's no comparison. Mostly a nice guy. But when he got riled up, he was a handful. First contact I recall having with your church involved him. And Louise."

"What happened?"

Lewis touched the nearest filing cabinet. "The case is old enough that the records have been archived at the island headquarters in Victoria. So, I don't have all the details here. But I'll tell you what I remember. Got a call... Must have been ten, eleven in the morning. Attend at St. Michael's and St. Joan's Catholic Church. It was a disturbance call. I arrived to find Louise and Gordon Joe just screaming their heads off at the priest. I remember he was a black guy with a thick accent, like maybe from the Caribbean or Africa. He had just arrived and was confused as hell. Gordon was demanding to know where the former priest was. Said they had some outstanding grievances they'd been addressing with him and the archbishop. The reason I remember so well is that Gordon had smashed one of the windows."

Barrett started, remembering the broken window in the vestry.

"You remember Shady Acres?"

"You mean that little collection of holiday cottages

out by the lake?" Barrett nodded. "The ones Squatch used to break into?"

"Yep. Those are the ones. Anyway, Gordon and Louise kept bringing them up. Not sure why. But I managed to defuse the situation. Got the priest to promise to follow up with the bishop. That seemed to pacify the Joes. Didn't deal with them again for about a year. Funny thing, though…"

"What?"

"When I *did* bump into Louise, I asked how things were going at church. She said she hadn't been in over a year. And she was planning never to go back."

Lewis yawned and stretched.

"I never did find out why," he concluded.

Plumbers

"FATHER BARRETT!"

"Archbish-...er, *Andrew.*" Barrett pressed the cell-phone against his ear with one shoulder as he set the file box in the rear of the Hyundai. "Good to hear from you. Allow me just one moment, if you please."

"Of course."

Barrett turned just as Danny Robert emerged from the church doorway, a file box under each arm. They had spent the morning sorting through and boxing up church records from the 1990 to 2000 era. It was time for these to go into the parish storage unit down on Crowley Street. Barrett grappled the keys for the Hyundai from his pants pocket.

"Hey, Danny." He smiled, embarrassed. "Got the Archbishop on the phone here. He needs to talk. Can you...?"

"No problem, father." Danny accepted the keys with a grin. "I'll drop these off, take care of setting up the bulletins and hymnals for Sunday, and then...see you tomorrow?"

"Let's do it. Say eleven AM?"

"I'll be there, father. And thanks."

"No, thank *you*." Barrett lifted the phone to his ear and watched as Danny piled the boxes in and closed the hatchback. "I'm back," he said quietly to Crowe. "Just getting Danny set with some tasks."

"How's he working out?"

"Fantastic. Can I adopt him?"

Crowe laughed. "I'm afraid not, Father Barrett. I have plans for that young priest. He's going to play a very important role in the future of our diocese."

"Then the future is bright, Andrew." Barrett looked up as Kelly Ward drove by, slowing her VW Beetle long enough to toss a wave through the window before motoring on to the community center. There was another meeting today that Barrett planned to attend.

"Mike, remember I mentioned that I might need your help for a, uh, *discreet* matter?"

"I remember. Yes."

"I'd like to meet privately." Barrett heard some papers shuffling and a muffled voice in the background—not Crowe's. Then: "Do you know Driftwood Bay?"

"The resort?" Barrett was familiar with the upscale vacation destination. "Yeah. It's just up the inside passage a short way from Campbell River."

"We'll meet there. The day after tomorrow. I've chartered a floatplane and will leave Vancouver at nine AM. Should arrive shortly before ten. We'll meet and talk and then I'll treat you to lunch."

"That would be very generous of you, Archbishop. Thanks."

"Hm." Crowe seemed to hesitate. "And how're the AA meetings going? You getting along alright with Reverend Ward?"

"Yes, Andrew." Barrett smiled quietly to himself. "Reverend Ward and I are getting along beautifully."

———————

HE ARRIVED on foot a few minutes after the meeting had started. Per protocol, he entered quietly and took a seat in the circle. A new member was speaking, relaying their experiences to the room. Everyone sat silent, listening without judgment. Including Kelly, who slid a glance and smirk his way as he took a seat. Barrett noted she was dressed like him today—conservatively, in priest mode. It suited her. She looked good in the black shirt and collar, blazer and polished black cowboy boots she was wearing. She looked…

…*hot*…

…extremely polished and professional. They shared a long, warm look before turning their attention to the woman speaking. She spoke of her troubles at home, with her husband, how she was forced to walk on eggshells around him. So she drank. She felt on the knife edge between killing herself with alcohol and being murdered by her husband. It was an extremely grim and unsettling story. But one heard many such tales in Twelve-Step meetings. That it was all confidential and kept within the walls of this room made the telling all the more heart-wrenching to hear.

In the silence following the woman's story, a voice said: "It's reassuring to see members of the clergy present."

Kelly and Barrett looked at each other and laughed. Although it wasn't customary to banter in the setting, nobody seemed to mind when she said: "Priests are people, too. We're no better. We just have a different job."

Barrett was nodding. "That's very true," he allowed.

"Priests are like plumbers," Kelly explained to the group. "We take our water for granted while it's flowing but once it shuts off, man do we have a problem. Plumber comes and fixes it. He helps. But he's not the source of the water."

Barrett chuckled. She had an entertaining way of expressing herself. And she was right. His quiet affirmation caught Kelly's attention and she smiled. And Barrett felt warmer and closer to her than he ever had before.

Another long silence fell. It broke when the voice whispered:

"You two should get married."

Barrett and Kelly exploded in peals of laughter. So did everybody else. It lasted a full minute but when it was over, they got back to recovery business.

―――――

"THAT WAS A GOOD MEETING!" Kelly stretched and craned up to look at the sky. They were walking together in the field behind the community center. When Barrett produced his cigarettes and offered her one, she took it, bent to the lighter and said:

"You're having a bad influence on me, Mike."

"Says the AA sponsor who invites her sponsee over for drinks and wrasslin'…"

"Hey, I counsel in my own way. And you're just sore cuz I *beatchya* wrasslin'."

"Did not."

"Did too."

Now they were laughing, walking side by side,

relaxing into one another's company like old friends or members of the same family. That's how it felt to Barrett, at any rate.

"Did you hear her? She said we should get married." He purposely said it without looking at her.

"Well, convert and we can." She elbowed his ribs.

"I could never marry a non-Catholic. You convert." He grinned. "You'd have to stop being a priest, of course."

"Assume my proper station? Mike, you know me better than that."

He did. He also knew her typical wardrobe. "You clean up nice," he commented. "Almost like a real priest."

"Gee, thanks," she said. "I'm doing some bereavement counseling for a parishioner."

"Hospice?"

"Yeah. They have this unit in the quiet part of the second floor of the hospital. It's in this unused ward. That's where they put the terminal cases."

"I ministered to a guy there a while back. Arnold McLellan."

"Not the easiest part of our job, is it?"

"Nope."

A low wall appeared ahead. More like a heap of tumbled bricks, grass had grown over top of the mound, furnishing a handy soft cover for a seat. Kelly found a place and sat. Barrett joined her.

"So what's your story, Kelly?" Barrett surprised himself by how urgent the question sounded coming from his lips. "How did you make the journey from judo champ to the Pats to the pulpit?"

Her cigarette hung a few inches from her lips. She had been raising it to her lips when she hesitated, considering Barrett's question. She narrowed her eyes and completed the gesture, bringing the cigarette to her lips and wrapping her lips around it. Barrett saw a small trace of lipstick stain the filter.

"Okay, so I was doing okay in high school. Excelling at judo. And I fell in with the wrong crowd." She grimaced, remembering. "People I thought were my friends. But they just brought me bad places. I got into fights. One landed me in front of a judge. I was an angry kid, Mike."

"Why?"

"Mm. Lotsa' things. Dad problems. Self-control issues. But mostly it's a lot of the same things that make me angry now. Injustice. Unfairness. Dishonesty."

"A lot of the same things that drove me to be a cop. Is that why you went Forces?"

"It seemed like a way to help. A way to make the world a better place. I joined and I loved it. The discipline. The camaraderie. Were the cops like that?"

"Sure." He laughed, smoke streaming from his lips. "Uniforms. Marching around. Saluting and yelling 'yes, sir' and 'no, ma'am.' Same idea. Uniting people into a team. But it's good. We're all working together toward a common goal of protecting and serving the public. Or, at least, that's how it *was*."

"So why the move from Toronto police to the church?"

Barrett swallowed. It was a period of life he rarely revisited, one he had discussed only once. But here he was making friends with another priest. So, he fought back his natural reticence and chose disclosure.

"My father stopped talking to me when I joined the police," he said. "It was, like, the ultimate betrayal for him, right? Most kids rebel from straight parents by becoming bohemians. I rebelled from organized crime by becoming a cop. And that was it. I was free of him. We didn't talk for five years. Then I got a call from one of his associates. My father was dying. Bone cancer."

"That's one of the worst types." The flat tone in which she said this affirmed she knew what she was talking about.

"Yeah. I arranged to go and see him. And the sight of a man who had been so powerful and brutal in life lying shrunken and terrified on that hospital bed put everything in perspective for me." Barrett shivered slightly as he spoke. He had never said this part out loud before. "And he *knew*. Absolutely knew that he was facing some kind of reckoning."

"But you said it was perspective. How did it shift the perspective for *you?*"

"The perspective for me was…I suppose confirmation that some sort of divine justice is at work in the universe." He stubbed out his cigarette and leaned forward, elbows on his knees, hands folded together and bumping his chin. "Why would God deliver that kind of agony on my father? His pain and suffering were terrible. But at the same time, it seemed absolutely appropriate. I took no pleasure watching him in agony. But the agony seemed warranted. Deserved, even. Like it was…*natural*. I can't express it any other way."

"I think I understand what you mean."

"I don't sound like a monster?"

She clapped his shoulder. "You don't."

They rose together and simply, naturally, wrapped an arm around each other as they began walking back through the field toward the community center.

"I won't lie," he said. "It feels good touching you."

"We don't get enough private, intimate touch in this line of work."

"We don't."

"I...like touching you, too, Mike."

A long, comfortable silence ensued. It ended when she stopped and pulled him closer. Not in an intimate way but with one hand on his jacket lapel and the other gripping Barrett's sleeve at the elbow. The classic judo stance. Barrett, familiar with the art, mirrored her.

"You actually would make a good sparring partner," she said, pulling him off-balance slightly.

"Oh, likewise."

Their eyes locked and then suddenly they were off, pushing and yanking each other, working for the throw. After a minute or so they stopped, panting breathlessly through laughter, their foreheads pressed against each other.

"I like you, Mike."

"I like you, too, Kelly."

Through sweat and panting, they watched each other.

"Friendship," he said. "Another thing we don't get enough of."

"Agreed."

Their faces were close together. She tilted her nose a little to the left. Their lips were lined up. They could touch. All either of their had to do was move a few inches closer.

Their eyes locked. Probing. Watching. Daring.

It was Barrett who broke the spell. He moved an inch or so away but, without releasing her, said, "I want to. So much. But I respect you, Kelly. And I respect what's developing between us too much. To..."

"To what?"

He smiled. "To rush."

She released him, grinning. "Your stock just shot up about 200 points, Barrett."

They hugged and returned to the community center before going their separate ways. A block from home, his cellphone buzzed. It was a text from Kelly.

For the record, I don't consider friends with benefits to be off the table.

Barrett replied:

Neither do I.
WALTON

Driftwood Bay resort, Google assured Barrett, was "among the premier recreational waterfront resorts in Western Canada." The pictures on their website were certainly impressive. Condo-style resort cottages dotted a grassy waterfront property with multiple boathouses and a float plane dock. With units renting at $500 per night, it definitely seemed like the sort of place for upscale holi-daymakers: doctors, lawyers and political operatives. Barrett thought it unlikely he'd bump into anyone making less than six figures per year.

"I've got to go meet with Archbishop Crowe," Barrett told Danny Robert as they sat together the next morning drinking coffee in the rectory kitchen.

"Uh-oh!" Danny Robert grinned teasingly. "You're not in trouble are you, father?"

Barrett chuckled. "I hope not. No, he needs to talk about some confidential matters, but he hasn't disclosed to me yet what they are."

"Confidential. But hasn't told you what they are."

Danny Robert's lips curled down at the edges and he nodded knowingly. "Yeah, you're in trouble."

Barrett laughed. In addition to being the dream deacon, Danny Robert was turning out to be very pleasant company. Attentive, thoughtful, humorous, and hard-working, Danny was great and Barrett could not have hoped for a better deacon.

"Let's hope not," he said. "Meantime, I'd like you to chair tomorrow's meeting of the parish working group…"

"No problem, father."

"I should be back in time for evening services." Barrett checked his watch. "I'm supposed to get there by ten AM. Hopefully we should only be a few hours."

"Where are you meeting, father?"

"Driftwood Bay Resort."

Danny let out a low whistle. "Wow. His excellency isn't sparing any expense, is he?"

"Yeah," grumbled Barrett. "I'll be rubbing shoulders with a bunch of rich people. Not my favorite thing to do."

Danny Robert nodded. Barrett could imagine how someone from the First Nations could probably feel the same way.

"Probably not a lot of Indians there, either," said Barrett.

Danny shrugged. "Maybe working in the kitchen," he said. "First Nations people and resorts don't usually mix."

———

THAT COMMENT STAYED WITH HIM. He recalled Gavin's story about intervening at the church when the priest had been confronted and Danny Robert's story about how his grandmother and other First Nations had stopped attending shortly after that. And how the tribal elders got very quiet whenever the issue was brought up.

Whatever happened must have been bad, he thought.

He would have to take care of buying essentials today as tomorrow would see him on the road. That meant he would have to handle his trip to the liquor store today. So once Danny left to attend to his duties, Barrett went for a walk to the strip mall where he bought his boxed wine. He nodded to the woman who was usually behind the register and wandered down the row that housed his favorite brand. He was reaching for a box when a voice spoke.

"Father Barrett, hello."

He looked up and saw the Chief of the local tribe. With his shorts and sandals, eyeglasses, and green base-ball cap, the Chief was a familiar and friendly sight. Barrett had dealt with the man on several occasions and held him in great respect. Low-key and self-effacing, he nevertheless had a mind like a steel trap and was fiercely protective of his people.

"Hi, Chief." Barrett straightened, a box of wine dangling from his arm. "Didn't expect to see you here."

"It's my granddaughter's birthday party." The Chief held up two large bottles of Coca-Cola. "Experience has taught me that's it's never wise to have a bunch of teenagers in the house without a supply of chips and soda."

"Good thinking." He accompanied the Chief to the register.

"How's Danny Robert working out for you?" The Chief's voice warmed with a kind of paternal pride. "We're all very excited to see our local boy made good."

"Danny is simply fantastic." Barrett shook his head. "I can basically leave the parish in his hands while I attend to other duties. He's been extremely helpful."

"That's great!" The Chief put his purchases on the counter and pulled out his wallet. "We think it's a good thing for more First Nations people to work in positions of responsibility, like the RCMP and government and the church. It's good to see you and Father—I mean, *Archbishop* Crowe giving Danny a chance."

The clerk rang up the Chief's items and bagged them.

"Do you remember when Crowe was the parish priest, Chief?"

"I do." The Chief nodded. "Many of the Otter People attended church back in those days. It was a good thing. Me, I like church. The same way I like the drumming in the longhouse. People coming together in spirit. It's a good thing."

The clerk rang up Barrett's wine box and handed over the receipt.

"I'm sad to hear that you guys attended church 'back then' but not now." Barrett picked up his wine. "Perhaps with Danny Robert joining, we can start to get more of you back in the door. What do you think, Chief?"

"I wouldn't mind," said the Chief. "But I think some reconciliation would have to happen first."

Barrett raised his eyebrows.

"Let's talk about it sometime," the Chief said. "I can fill you in on some history."

"I'd appreciate that very much, Chief."

The old man smiled. "You take care, father," he said. Then he picked up his bottles of soda and left.

———

HE WAS about a block from home when the sound of shrieking tires rose and Gavin Lewis' Crown Victoria barreled around the corner, lights flashing. Lewis braked to a halt beside Barrett and he could tell at once something was horribly wrong. Lewis was shaken, clearly fighting to maintain his self-control as he rolled down the passenger window.

"Padre…"

"Gavin." Barrett stepped over and put his hand on the windowsill. "What's going on?"

"Break-in. At Logan's Sporting Goods. Mike…"

"What is it?"

"It's Adam! Walton. I think he's hurt!"

Barrett hauled open the passenger door and got in. "Punch it," he said. And Gavin floored it, hauling the wheel and fishtailing onto the main drag.

Logan's Sporting Goods was Fulton's one-stop shop for all things hunting and fishing related. The place did booming business, operating twelve hour-long shifts during the weekend but limited hours during the week. Dave Logan and his wife Sally took their days of rest during the week. Today was a day when the store was closed.

There was nothing notable about the closed shop front, so Lewis sped down the alleyway beside the brick building to the rear. Walton's Conservation Service truck was parked there. Barrett could see the back door of the shop was open and one of the rear windows was broken.

A trail of blood led from Walton's truck into the store.

"Jesus," whispered Lewis. "Here, padre." He handed over his Sig Sauer and unclipped the C8 assault rifle from between the seats. "We're going in."

Barrett swallowed. "Okay," he said, checking the load on the automatic. "Let's do this."

They rolled out of the Crown Vic, guns up, advancing on the rear of the building. Barrett flattened himself against the wall to one side of the entrance while Lewis advanced, sighting into the store, the beam from the C8's combat flashlight knifing into the gloom within. Barrett noted the trail of blood crossing the threshold, and a bloody handprint on the doorjamb.

"Clear," whispered Lewis. He edged forward into Logan's. Barrett raised the Sig Sauer and followed. The rear door opened onto a long, narrow hallway. At the end of the hallway was the service entrance to the sales floor. Halfway between the rear door and the sales floor entrance was the opening to the stock room. Reaching it, they followed the same routine, with Barrett hugging the wall while Lewis went in, scanning with the C8.

"Jesus…"

Barrett hurried in. Expecting to find a wounded Walton, he was surprised to find the policeman standing over a crate that had been jimmied open.

"Look at this," Lewis whispered.

Barrett stepped up beside him and peered down. The crate was constructed with racks to hold hunting rifles. There were enough spaces for eight…

Three were missing.

"Come on." Lewis sounded panicky. "We'd best find Adam."

They spilled back out into the hallway, headed for the sales floor, weapons hot. Lewis panned back and forth with the C8's light. There was another red handprint on the wall and the trail of blood on the floor continued.

Voices. Out on the sales floor! They heard Walton:

"FREEZE! Hands in the air! Now now now!"

Something crashed that sounded like the front door being smashed open. Then Lewis and Barrett were running to reach the sales floor. Walton cried out again. He snapped off a shot from his service pistol and then...

BOOM!

The blast of a heavy bore hunting rifle crashed, echoing off the walls. Lewis rushed forward, Barrett right behind him. Walton lay crumpled on the floor, a fast-spreading pool of blood beneath him. Lewis fired a blast from the C-8 in the direction of the door, then stood between Walton and the door as Barrett knelt beside the fallen Conservation Officer.

He set the Sig Sauer down and turned Walton over. A chunk of his left shoulder was gone, the fabric of his jacket there shredded and smoldering from the impact of the round. Rifles like the ones that had been taken fire high-grain bullets designed to take down large deer and similar game. The impact on a human was gruesome and violent in the...

Get ahold of yourself man!

He began checking vitals. Walton was still breathing, albeit very shallowly. His pulse was faint and fluttery. He needed blood plasma, a surgical team and antibiotics. Barrett had none of those things. So, he held Walton's hand and waited as the sound of an approaching ambulance siren wailed in the distance.

———

"HE'S LOST A LOT OF BLOOD."

The doctor stood in her soiled surgical scrubs, face mask dangling from one ear, leaning against the waiting room door, exhausted after two hours of emergency surgery.

"The bullet sheared away most of his collar bone and ripped through the flesh, exposing the shoulder socket in a compound wound." She sighed. "I'm not going to lie. A few inches south and you'd be talking to a mortician right now, not a surgeon. He's alive, but he's far from out of the woods. I've put him in a medically-induced coma as a counter to late onset shock. He's going to be under for a while. I give him about a sixty percent chance of survival."

Lewis stood ramrod straight, his face expressionless. He listened to the doctor, nodded his thanks and marched out to the parking lot. Barrett followed him.

"I know who did it, padre."

"You're thinking it's the Messiah?"

"Who else?" Lewis' breathing betrayed his rage. "The escalating crime in this town, attacks coming more frequently and bloodier by the day. He may not have been in there, but he sure as hell ordered the break-in. Now my partner's been shot."

Lewis paused, panting heavily.

"Gavin." Barrett placed a hand on the cop's arm. "Take it easy, man."

"I'm going to kill the son-of-a-bitch, padre."

"Vengeance is mine, sayeth the Lord."

"*FUCK THAT!*" Lewis jerked his arm away. "Vengeance may be God's. But I'm sure as hell gonna help myself to a big goddam chunk of it before this is all over!"

With that, he climbed into his Crown Victoria, slammed the door, and sped away.

Driftwood Bay

BARRETT SLOWED the Hyundai and turned into the parking lot of the Driftwood Bay holiday resort shortly before 10 AM the next morning. There was a guard hut at the edge of the lot manned by smartly uniformed parking attendants, one of whom stepped out and beamed a grin at Barrett that was annoyingly bright.

"Good morning, sir! And welcome to Driftwood Bay! My name is Danny! And with your permission, I'd be happy to park your vehicle for you!"

Barrett squinted against the noise. *Jesus, does he have to broadcast every sentence like a baseball announcer?* He studied the dusty and cluttered dash of the Hyundai, jammed with empty cigarette packs, fast food napkins, gas receipts and old church bulletins. If Danny *(Danny!)* wanted to park the thing for him, so be it. Barrett let himself out and handed over the keys.

"Thank you!" Danny pointed to an electric golf cart parked at the edge of a path that wound through trees. "My colleague DeeDee will be pleased to convey you to the reception desk!"

"Great..." Barrett shuffled over to the cart, where he was greeted by a smartly uniformed, brazenly grinning female attendant.

"Good morning, sir! Welcome to Driftwood Bay! My name is DeeDee!" She held out a steaming basket. "May I offer you a warm towel?"

"No thanks. I ate already."

DeeDee *(DeeDee!)* set down the basket, engaged the clutch and guided the electric cart up the path, which undulated through a picturesque forest and then up a rise to the imposing entrance of the Driftwood Bay "visitor center." It looked like the kind of monstrosity the British might have constructed during their occupation of India. DeeDee dropped him off at the foot of the steps leading into the foyer. Barrett slogged into the air-conditioned lobby and crossed to the registration desk.

"Hi. I'm Father Mike Barrett. I'm here to see Archbishop Crowe."

The desk clerk, whose nametag identified him as 'Bruce' *(Bruce!)* smiled toothily and hit a few keys on his computer. "Father Barrett! Yes! We have the archbishop's room reservation." He scanned the screen. "He's asked us, in the event you arrive first, to notify you when he arrives."

"Uh, yeah? Okay..." Barrett frowned, confused. "Is, ah, the Archbishop...?"

"The Archbishop hasn't checked in yet! But we'll notify you when he does!"

"Great." Barrett nodded. "I'll be in the bar."

He made his way into the darkened, peaceful mahogany-lined lounge and slumped onto a barstool with relief. The bartender was an older man with an Ernest Hemingway-type beard. Barrett liked the guy already.

"So. What's your name?" Barrett grimaced as he produced a pack of smokes and lit up.

"David, sir. What's your pleasure?"

"Gimme a martini. And a glass of Coca-Cola on the side. Also…do you have any breath mints?"

"Never fear, sir." David the bartender set a dish of mints on the bar before him. "We care for all our customers' needs."

"Well, hot damn." Barrett popped one into his mouth. "The Coke is camouflage in case my boss appears."

"Very fine, sir." David smiled. "Do you prefer gin or vodka for your martini?"

"Both."

"Done." David immediately bent to chopping ice. Barrett admired the guy's skills. He was a dab hand with a measuring cup and shaker. Before Barrett knew it, David had set the strainer atop a martini glass and was pouring out the clear elixir. "One olive or two, sir?"

"Two please. It's almost lunchtime."

"Right you are, sir." David speared two olives on a plastic swizzle sword, lowered them into the glass, which he set on a napkin, and pushed across the bar.

Barrett took a deep whiff of the fumes before closing his eyes for a first sip. The martini was chilly and smooth and oh-so-deliciously good. He drank, smoked, and chomped olives contentedly until David appeared with a telephone.

"Call for you, sir."

Barrett finished off the martini, popped two mints into his mouth and picked up the receiver.

"Sir? This is Bruce at the registration desk! The Archbishop has arrived! He says he'll meet you for lunch in the main dining room in fifteen minutes!"

Barrett winced, holding the phone away from his ear as he absorbed Bruce's announcement. Then he thanked him and hung up.

"Why does everybody that works here speak at the top of their lungs, David?"

"Company culture, sir. The management likes a happy, welcoming crew."

"I notice you don't."

"I'm the bartender, sir. Nobody tells the bartender what to do."

"Nice." Barrett sucked on his Coke. "Maybe I'm in the wrong line of work."

"I see you're a priest," David noted. "I suspect we hear about the same number of confessions."

BARRETT WANDERED into the dining room, carrying his Coca-Cola. The Archbishop was waiting for him at a table. Crowe smiled as Barrett entered, rose and extended a hand.

"Thank you for coming, Michael," he said. "I trust you had a pleasant drive?"

"Pleasant enough, your excellency," Barrett said. "And your flight?"

"Smooth." Crowe smiled, gesturing for Barrett to have a seat. "Floatplanes are always so much easier on the body than takeoffs and landings in conventional aircraft. I hope you brought a good appetite. The waiter just informed me they have fresh salmon."

"Salmon, eh?" Barrett smiled queasily. "I'm not much of a fish guy, your ex-....ah, Andrew. I'd be happier with a hamburger steak."

"I'm sure that can be managed." Crowe glanced at

the Coke. "Glad to see you're not drinking. Things continuing to go well with our friend Reverend Ward?"

"Quite well," Barrett said. And figured it was probably best to leave things at that.

The waiter came and took their orders. Barrett opted for a filet mignon and a refill on his Coke.

"Well!" Crowe reached under his glasses, rubbed his eyes and sat back, allowing a generous smile to rest on Barrett. "I must say, it's a pleasure to have a chance to talk in a way that's both informal and confidential. As senior princes of the Church, we're expected to keep a certain distance from our subordinates. But I've always been curious to know you a bit better. You've had quite the career. Working for the Curia as an investigator... That must have been quite fascinating."

"Uh, well... Really, there were a lot of meetings and memos." Barrett paused. "It was like working for any large organization. At a certain level, you leave behind operational reality for a fog of management theory. Like working for the world's biggest corporation. Which, really, we are. If you think about it."

"Father Barrett, you surprise me! The Catholic Church was founded by our Lord. *'Upon this rock...'* You *do* believe that don't you?"

"Of course, Andrew. But if human history is any indication, Man has a great track record of screwing up pretty much anything God creates. We're great at that..."

"I suppose we are." Crowe paused as the waiter brought their salad course. "I'm sure not denying that the Church has occasionally fallen into error. Most certainly, we have had bishops and Popes who have done so. Like Pope Alexander and his brood of illegitimate children by several mistresses. Popes who promoted war or incorrect doctrine. But organizations can't repent. Only people can."

Crowe appeared to hesitate. Then:

"Like me, for instance," he concluded.

Barrett felt the breath leave his body. As a priest, he was trained to view his superiors as embodiments and ambassadors of Divine truth. Not infallible, exactly, but certainly not to be questioned. Expressions of self-doubt from an archbishop were not on any priest's bingo card. But here they were. And now Crowe was talking again.

"I was ambitious," he said simply. "Even as a newly ordained priest, I had my eyes on higher office. I've always been that way, Mike. I guess I feel like I have a...*perspective* that lends itself to guiding others from on high. It's not ego. It's more like...a talent, I suppose. And I knew I had it from the beginning."

"Well, that's good." Barrett shrugged. "You wanted to put that to the service of the Church, and your ambition helped make it happen. Thanks be to God." He toasted Crowe with his soda. "Better you than me. I have no talent that way."

"Kind of you to say." Crowe nodded. "I had to make compromises, of course. Cut some corners. And look the other way. Sometimes." He chose his words carefully. "My ambition did not go unnoted, particularly by my superior at the time. Archbishop Radcliffe encouraged my ambitions and even set me to work on some tasks on his behalf. It wouldn't be until some years down the road that I would understand how some of those tasks were neither entirely appropriate nor ethical. But, as is often the case, the partnership bound us on both a personal and professional level."

"Archbishop Radcliffe was guilty of wrongdoing?"

"Not my place to say." Crowe held up his hands.

"But under his tutelage, my elevation from priest to bishop occurred quite swiftly. A certain warmth and collegiality grew up between us. Shared obligations will do that between men. It also means that I now find myself in the position of needing your help." Crowe swallowed. "The archbishop has been forced by circumstances to move out of his present quarters in a parochial house. I've arranged for him to be lodged elsewhere, but there will be a short delay. I was wondering…if he could live with you."

"With *me?*"

"Just for a few days." Crowe laid a hand on Barrett's arm. "You have a spare room at the rectory. Just move him in there for a while. Have Miss Dolan make extra portions for breakfast and lunch. And the moment his new quarters become available I'll take him off your hands. I promise."

Barrett considered this. He was, in all honesty, a deeply anti-social creature. But Crowe's request, in light of the circumstances he'd outlined, was not only reasonable but also compassionate. It really wasn't much of a request.

"Does the Archbishop have any special medical needs I should be aware of?" he asked.

Crowe seemed to relax a bit at the question. "Well, he's quite aged. And as you can probably imagine, he faces all the usual complaints that come with that privilege. But he has no serious physical issues. No mobility or chronic pain issues. Nothing like that."

Why do I sense a 'but' coming? Barrett thought.

"There are challenges," Crowe admitted. He spoke as if steeling himself to admit unpleasant truths. "Some of the Archbishop's errors in judgment had a very direct impact on your parish and the people in it. This was decades ago, mind. But one challenge you will have to face is keeping his presence quiet. We want to move him in, keep him under wraps. For the moment. That's one obstacle you'll be forced to deal with."

"Okay…"

Crowe sighed. "I should perhaps also mention—"

A great crash sounded from the lobby, like someone dropping a tray full of dishes onto a brick floor. The silence following the crash was punctuated by a single, bright "ha!"

"…should also mention that his mental faculties, while always impressive, seem to have deteriorated somewhat in old age."

"You mean he's bonkers," Barrett said flatly.

"That's a very uncharitable characterization, Father Barrett…"

More noise and commotion. Someone was creating a disturbance at the dining room entrance. Two waitresses were running interference to try and prevent an elderly man in housecoat and slippers from entering the dining room.

"Please, sir… You're not properly—"

"Sir, you can't come in here like that—"

"*HA!*"

"Oh, goodness." Crowe rose, wiped his lips with his napkin and stepped toward the door. "I see he's about to join us. Just give me a second, Mike."

Radcliffe

BARRETT WATCHED HELPLESSLY as Crowe scuttled across the dining room and wrapped an arm around the elderly man's shoulders. The two waitresses appeared to relax. Crowe, putting on his best PR smile, turned to them and began a complex and, apparently, very funny explanation for Radcliffe's behavior because soon the waitresses were laughing. Crowe took the opportunity to steer Radcliffe away toward the table. The aged Archbishop accompanied his successor, grinning vacantly, probing the ceiling for…

For what? Barrett wondered. *What's he looking for up there? Birds? Aliens?*

"Father Barrett! Allow me to introduce an old friend. This is His Excellency, Archbishop Leonard Radcliffe." Crowe beamed at the elderly cleric.

Barrett rose. "Your excellency, how do you do?" he said, extending a hand.

Radcliffe, who up to then had been fiddling with his housecoat's sash, looked up, a weird light springing to life in his eyes. He noticed Barrett's hand, threw his head back, and answered:

"Ha!"

"Okay…" Barrett withdrew his hand and flashed a watery smile. He hoped the facial expression he turned to Crowe didn't seem too desperate. "Well, shall we continue our lunch?"

"Lunch?" exclaimed Radcliffe. "Ha!"

"Come and sit, Leonard. There's a good fellow." Crowe gentled Radcliffe into a chair, then said to Barrett: "As you can see, the archbishop still hasn't lost his sense of humor."

"No," said Barrett mildly, unfolding a napkin. "He seems to find humor in the…well, slightest things…"

"A very healthy quality!" Crowe said as the waiter arrived with their main course.

"Will the other gentleman be joining you for lunch?" he asked, setting down their meals.

"Yes," said Crowe. "I'd like to see your children's menu. If you've got one."

———

IT TURNED out that Crowe had brought Radcliffe fully packed for a stay with Barrett. With the Archbishop's two large suitcases stowed in the Hyundai's rear seat, Barrett nervously took his place in the driver's spot alongside his new houseguest. The former prince of the church was rolling the window up and down while making what were (apparently) motorboat noises with his mouth.

"If you run into any difficulty," Crowe said, leaning at the window, "don't hesitate to call."

"Sure," said Barrett, offering another watery smile.

"Leonard? Leonard!" Crowe leaned in at the window. "You be on your best behavior now…"

"Ha!"

Barrett decided that, once they returned to Fulton, he might borrow one of Lewis's guns and shoot himself.

He had just turned out of the driveway when his cellphone rang. He pulled over and checked caller ID. It was Danny Robert. Barrett decided to answer.

"Father, hello. Just thought to check in and make sure everything is okay."

"Thank you, Danny. We're fine. Um…" He looked over at Radcliffe, who had abruptly fallen asleep and was now snoring softly. "Looks like we'll be having company at the parish house. His excellency has asked me to take in a houseguest. I may, um, need your help with him…"

"Certainly, father. Whatever you need. May I ask…who?"

"Ah. The former archbishop. Archbishop Radcliffe."

Hearing his name, the old cleric woke, muttered a muted "*ha!*" then fell back to sleep.

"We should be home in a few hours."

There was a long pause. Then Danny Robert said: "Have a safe trip, father." And hung up.

———

"BATHROOM!"

"I'm sorry, your excellency?"

"Bathroom! *Bathroom!*"

Barrett gritted his teeth and took the next off-ramp. There was a rest-stop a quarter mile up the highway. No sooner had they pulled over than Radcliffe was reefing open the door and sprinting for the men's washroom. Barrett exited the car, stretched and lit a cigarette just as his cellphone rang. He checked the caller ID...

And grinned.

"Hello, Kelly."

"Hey, Mike." He could hear her voice swell around a smile. "Just wanted to call and see how your trip's going."

"On my way back now." He checked his watch. "Should be another hour or so."

"How was Driftwood Bay?"

"They make excellent martinis."

"As your AA sponsor, I'll pretend I didn't hear that." She giggled. "Listen, I stopped by the hospital to check on your friend Adam, the Conservation Officer."

"How's he doing?"

"No change. But the prosthesis specialist was in. He says Adam qualifies for a prosthetic shoulder. With some therapy he should regain about 70% functionality of rotation."

"Assuming he ever wakes up!"

"He will, Mike. We'll both pray on it."

"Thank you." He swallowed before adding: "I want to see you."

"I want to see you, too. Call me when you get back?"

"Count on it."

They said their goodbyes and hung up. A short time later, Radcliffe came shambling out of the washroom. "All better?" asked Barrett.

"Ha!"

"Wonderful. Buckle up. Let's go."

IT WAS GROWING dark by the time they pulled into the driveway. It wasn't until Barrett switched off the car that he noticed the change in Radcliffe. The elderly Archbishop was suddenly subdued, watchful. And, for the first time since Barrett had met him, fully aware of his surroundings.

"Where...?" Radcliffe's voice trailed off, dropping the question.

"We're in Fulton, your excellency. Perhaps you...?"

But Radcliffe was opening the passenger door and stepping onto the driveway, peering around like a shelter dog that's just been rescued and brought to his new home. Watching him, Barrett felt a chill snarl his spine.

"Fulton," Radcliffe said quietly.

"That's right." Barrett stepped up next to him. "Do you remember Fulton, Archbishop Radcliffe?"

"The parish here..." Radcliffe paused. "St. Michael and St. Joan." He grinned, pleased with himself for remembering. "So, where's Andrew? He's the parish priest here!"

"Not anymore, your excellency. He's the Archbishop. These days, I'm the parish priest at St. Michael's and St. Joan's Catholic Church."

"You?" Radcliffe squinted. "Who are you again?"

"Father Michael Barrett, your excellency."

"Ha!"

Barrett fought down the urge to punch him. "Let's get you settled in the spare room."

———

IT TOOK SOME DOING. First of all, there were the two huge, heavy suitcases to lug upstairs. Radcliffe was of absolutely no help. And the bags were heavy enough that Barrett had to carry them up one at a time. Each one forced him to pause for rest before reaching the top.

What the hell's he got in these things? he wondered. *Cannonballs?* He considered posing the question to Radcliffe himself but was fairly sure he would receive the archbishop's favored monosyllabic response and so dropped the idea. He humped the bag into the guest room with its striped wallpaper, half bathroom and framed art prints and set it at the foot of the four-poster bed before returning for a second trip.

He passed Radcliffe in the kitchen. Several of the cupboards were open. The old man was piling canned goods onto the kitchen table. Barrett decided against an intervention just yet. He could replace the cans later. The first priority was getting the kook situated in a locale where he could do as little damage as possible. Barrett wondered if it was possible to rent straitjackets.

The second suitcase was even heavier than the first. It took Barrett three rest stops before reaching the top of the stairs and an arm-twisting, shoulder-deadening voyage down the second floor hallway before he could finally set it down. He reflected that housing Radcliffe in the guestroom was a good idea since it was a long and winding path from there to any other point in the house. The archbishop's own dementia would be his jailer.

Once I've got him in there with the door closed, he'll never find his way back, Barrett thought as he returned to the kitchen. He added triumphantly: *Ha!*

His good humor lasted until the moment he reached the stove.

"Your excellency, would you mind coming out from under the kitchen table, please?"

"Ha!"

"Okay, look." Barrett went to the sink and took down his box of wine from the cabinet. "Your being under the table is going to render conversation difficult, if not impossible. However, I *am* a gracious host…" He took his coffee mug from the dish drainer and filled it with wine. "If that's where you're comfortable for now, I'll allow it. But sooner or later you're going to have to start following house rules."

"Wine! Gimme wine!"

"Come out from under the table and I just might."

These words grabbed Radcliffe's attention like nothing else before. Barrett watched as the housecoat-and-pajama clad archbishop rolled to all fours and crawled out between the legs of the table. As he hauled himself up on the edge of the counter, Barrett grabbed the nearest container from the drinks cupboard, which happened to be someone's donated Mickey Mouse juice glass. *Perfect!* Barrett half-filled it and pressed it into Radcliffe's hands.

"A toast." Barrett raised his glass. "To your emergence from beneath the kitchen table."

"Ha!"

"Chin-chin."

They drank.

"Okay." Barrett wiped the back of his mouth. "We gotta' figure out how to get you squared away. I can't be here to babysit you full time. And my housekeeper is only here until about one or two in the afternoon. So, you'll be spending most of your time with my deacon."

"Deacon? Ha!"

"No, not ha-ha deacon. Deacon very serious deacon. And he'll be watching your loony ass. Because if *I* do it, I'm likely to end up strangling you." Barrett wandered to the utility drawer, hauled it open, and began pawing through its contents. *There!* Pushing aside a jar of screws, he hauled out a lock-ring and hasp set still enclosed within its plastic blister pack and a long, black-handled screwdriver. The final item, a combination lock, he placed on the counter beside the rest. Then he shut the drawer, resumed his wine and turned to Radcliffe.

"I'm thinking we're going to do a kind of halfway-house, work-release-type arrangement. You'll be free to wander around, uttering *ha!* To your heart's content when there's somebody to make sure you don't fall down a hole or set fire to something. But the moment they're gone, slam!"

"Slam?"

"'*To da room, Alice! To da room!*'" Barrett chuckled at his own poor imitation of Jackie Gleason's Ralph Kramden voice. Radcliffe seemed unmoved. "You will be confined to quarters, just like onboard a naval vessel. In the brig, archbishop. In the brig. Now, don't look at me like that... It's for your own good!"

"Ha!"

"It's either that or I raid the evidence locker down at the police station for something I can use to drug you." Barrett shrugged. "Which seems a little extreme, so we'll try it my way for now." He topped up Radcliffe's wine, gathered up the stuff on the counter and said: "Bring your drink, archbishop. And I'll show you to your room."

Radcliffe followed him upstairs and stood passively by, sipping boxed wine as Barrett installed the lock-ring and hasp on the guest room door. Then, ushering Radcliffe inside, Barrett closed the door behind him and secured it with the padlock.

"Night-night, your excellency!"

As he walked away, faintly from behind the door, he heard a single, timid: "Ha."

He was just cleaning up in the kitchen when the phone rang.

"Barrett here."

"Is this Father Barrett?" The voice at the other end was young and female. "Is Danny Robert there?"

"Uh, no. Danny's only here during the day. Evenings he spends at home with his family."

"This is his sister, Connie." The woman sounded worried. "Do you know where he is? He didn't come home tonight."

"No." Barrett was surprised. "I spoke to him earlier today. He didn't say anything about changing his work or housing plans."

"We're very worried," Connie said. "If you see him, will you get him to call home, please?"

"Of course, I will. No worries. We'll find out where your brother is." He hung up, visibly worried.

He sat up, tinkering with his sermon for a few hours. His final act, before going to bed, was to take out a pencil and paper and leave a note for Miss Dolan. He dropped it on the kitchen table before turning out the lights and heading to his room.

MISS DOLAN:

PLEASE DON'T BE ALARMED, BUT I HAVE AN ARCHBISHOP LOCKED IN THE GUEST ROOM. I'LL EXPLAIN EVERYTHING IN THE MORNING.

—FATHER BARRETT

Scooter

"AH, FATHER BARRETT. MIKE." Barrett could almost hear Crowe smile across the digital distance of their cellphone connection. "Sorry. I was on the other line when you called. It was Miss Dolan."

Barrett yawned, rolled over in bed and blinked at his bedroom window a half-dozen times before the words registered. He guessed the time at around 7 or 8 AM.

So! The perfidious Miss Dolan was already at work, undermining him by making panicked telephone calls to the Archbishop's office in Vancouver? He would put a stop to that shit at once!

"Oh? I wasn't aware Miss Dolan had your number, Andrew."

"Oh, she just has the main office number. She's been with us so long that, well, I sort of feel obliged to take her calls. If you know what I mean."

"Andrew… You're an *Archbishop*. You don't have to talk to anybody you don't want to."

"Nonsense, Michael. Being an Archbishop means

exactly having to talk to all sorts of people you don't want to talk to. It's the essence of the job."

"Ah. Well." Barrett shifted, trying to ease the pressure on his full bladder. "God's will be done, then."

"Precisely. Now. To business. Do you have Archbishop Radcliffe padlocked into your guest room?"

"Yes."

"Ah." There came a long pause. "Well, if you believe it's for the best…"

"He's got a washroom and free cable in there, Andrew. He'll be fine."

"I'll leave him to your discretion, Mike. But please don't be too hard on the old man. He's been through a lot."

"Yes, he certainly has put me through a lot. But that's neither here nor there. Andrew, I'm afraid Danny Robert has gone missing all of a sudden."

After a long, stunned silence, Crowe asked, "When did this happen?"

"Last night. I received a call from his sister saying he hadn't come home. I have a text here saying there's still been no sign of him."

"Well, go find him. For Pete's sake, Mike, he's our ordained. We're responsible for him. We can't just…*misplace* priests."

Barrett thought: *Misplaced priests…warehoused priests…priests locked in spare bedrooms…*

"It would be considered especially catastrophic if we lost such a promising, young ordained from the First Nations. The National Council would have to become involved. This would be a big problem for me, Mike."

"I understand, your excellency."

"Make it go away for me, Mike."

"Will do."

_____

"AH! FATHER!" As Barrett entered the kitchen, Miss Dolan dried her hands briskly and turned from the teacups she had been washing in the sink. "Now that you're finally up. What on *Earth* is going on with this note you sent me?" She produced the paper from an apron pocket and unfolded it with moist fingertips. "What's this nonsense? You have an *archbishop* locked in the guest room? And when I go to look, lo and behold there is a padlock on the *door*...? Father, what on Earth have you done?"

Barrett held up a hand. "Miss Dolan, until I've had my coffee, I shan't be answering any questions. To expect otherwise contravenes the Geneva Convention."

"The Geneva Convention only applies when we're at war, father. And we are not, at this moment in time."

"Nonsense, Miss Dolan. For what is human history but one long war of attrition against sin and evil?" He rummaged in the cupboards. "Did you remember to buy sugar?"

"It's in the blue bowl beside the tea pot, father. Now." She cleared her throat. "Might I ask? Please? Whether the archbishop you have locked up on the guest room mightn't be Archbishop Radcliffe?"

"Winner, winner, chicken dinner," Barrett mumbled, grappling the carafe from the coffee maker and going in search of his mug. "It is *indeed* our very dear, most learned Archbishop Radcliffe, formerly of the Archdiocese of Vancouver. Our dear archbishop has fallen upon most serious and grievous mental affliction in some form of early onset…wackiness. You can imagine the embarrassment to the Archdiocese should it ever become put about that its former head has devolved into a gibbering wackadoo."

"That's most uncharitable of you, father."

"Well, the modern media has shown a distinct inclination toward charity where reporting on the church is concerned. Which brings me back to my earlier theme of good and evil." Barrett poured some mud into his mug, took an experimental sip and sighed. "Embarrassing the church and our present Archbishop is, of course, completely unacceptable. I have agreed to take charge of his excellency as a personal favor to Archbishop Crowe, who is aware of the steps I have taken. He understands the, ah, *danger* that the Archbishop poses. Particularly to…" He paused and blinked dramatically. "Well, to available females."

She blanched noticeably. "I'm ever so glad you mentioned that, father. Still. I would feel a good deal better knowing he was alright. Can we look in on him?"

"Certainly."

Barrett led the way upstairs and along the corridor to the guest bedroom door. Arriving there, he dialed the padlock open and pulled it free. Then he knocked twice and pushed wide the door.

Fortunately, the sight was nothing shocking or scandalous. Radcliffe, his housecoat and pajamas straightened, was sitting up in bed watching television, the remote control on the pillow beside him. Every now and then he fished a potato chip from the bowl in his lap or took a swig from the beer on the bedside table.

"Your excellency!" Miss Dolan caught her breath. "Archbishop Radcliffe, I must say. Wasn't expecting to find you locked in our guest bedroom of a Wednesday morning!"

"You seem to have made yourself comfortable." Barrett noted a reality show playing on the flatscreen and an empty beer bottle beside the full one. "I didn't know we stock a wet bar in here, Miss Dolan."

"We don't, father."

"Ha!" Radcliffe sucked down more beer, then added, "That Indian kid brought it."

———

BARRETT'S first order of business was to find his missing deacon. But he didn't, for the life of him, have the slightest idea where to begin.

He wasn't going to bother Lewis. Not yet, anyway. The lawman had troubles enough of his own right now. Already overburdened with the wave of street-crime submerging the town, the Mountie also had concern for Walton weighing on his mind. No, Barrett decided he would exhaust the contacts within his church network before involving the RCMP. He decided to check on his parish.

There were no signs of life at the church when he arrived. Barrett let himself into the office and scanned around the small desk and work area he had set aside for Danny's use but it held no recent indications of his presence. There was no sign of Danny's blue nylon lunch pouch or vacuum-sealed water container in the office fridge. It was as if the ground had just opened and swallowed him up entirely.

Barrett muffled a grunt of frustration and exited by the side door. He followed the flagstone path around the parking lot behind the church. The vast lot with the faintly visible parking lines and cracked macadam surface was empty of a weekday morning. The only thing visible was an aged RV parked at the far end, moldering under the branches of Spanish Moss planted around the edge of the lot. Barrett approached and knocked twice on the door.

The trailer shook, footsteps rattling the flooring as its resident approached. The door opened and a narrow-faced man wearing a baseball cap stuck out his head.

"Hi, Scooter," said Barrett. "Got a minute?"

"Sure thing, father!" Scooter, the parish groundskeeper, grinned widely. "Was just about to pop open a beer. Care for one?"

"Don't mind if I do, thanks."

Scooter held open the door for Barrett. He entered, stepping around the snuffling, drooling form of Winston, Scooter's dog that had formerly been 'gifted' to Barrett by a departing member of his congregation. During his time in the rectory, he had snuffled and pissed on virtually every piece of furniture on the ground floor, sending Miss Dolan into hygienic hysterics. *Good times,* he thought with a grin. He nudged the miniature bulldog aside with a foot and took a seat on the padded circular bench in the kitchen nook. Scooter pulled two cans of Lucky from the fridge. With the shades drawn and soft lighting, the interior of the RV had the feel of a men's club, circa 1961. Soft jazz played on the stereo system: Coltrane's *Black Pearls*.

"Cheers!" Scooter held up his beer can. "How you been, padre?"

"Oh, alright." Barrett sipped cautiously. "Got a bit of a problem, Scooter. My deacon has gone missing."

"Danny's gone missing?" Scooter's surprise was palpable. "Sheesh! That's not like him at all!"

"I know it." Barrett spread his hands. "Everything was going along just fine. The guy was just about the most helpful parish assistant I've ever met. Much more helpful than I ever was after ordination. We spoke on the phone yesterday and that was the last I heard of him. Next thing I know, his sister is calling up wondering where's he gotten to."

"He was staying with his people on the rez, wasn't he?" Scooter rummaged in the cupboard for a bag of potato chips. "Because if he was in some sort of trouble, home is right there. First Nations are no different from the rest of us. When the world kicks our asses, ain't no place like home. Er, pardon my Anglo-Saxon, father…"

"No worries, Scooter." Barrett helped himself to a chip. "Do you know of any other places Danny might go for protection?"

"Well, really the Chief would be the guy to ask…" Scooter frowned and scratched his scalp. "I never knew Danny that well. Used to see him around town and suchlike. Back when he was a teenager. And I'll tell you what, father. He used to raise some *Hell*…"

"Gavin Lewis was mentioning something about that."

"Oh, *yeah!*" Scooter shook his head, remembering. "Man! If you had told me fifteen years ago that Danny Robert would grow up to be a Roman Catholic priest, I'd have told you to take off, eh? For a period of time, almost every single petty crime in this town had his name attached to it. Everything from shoplifting to smashed windows to graffiti – Danny got up to it at one point or another. He was a frequent flyer in the back of Sergeant Lewis' Crown Vic."

Danny Robert? Barrett's alarm assumed unwieldy

proportions. It was as if Scooter were talking about a completely different person.

"Why?" Barrett shook his head. "What was going on in his life that made him such a hard case? It just seems so completely out of character."

Scooter sighed. "I know his family was part of the Sasquatch clan."

"Wait. What?" Beneath Barrett's confusion bubbled a thread of amusement. "Sasquatch as in *'Bigfoot'*?"

"Oh, yeah." Scooter was dead serious. "He's no joke to the Indians, father. Every tribe on the island has stories about Sasquatch."

"So, who were the 'Sasquatch Clan'?"

"It's a nickname for ex-parishioners from here." Scooter gestured vaguely in the direction of the church. "Up until about twenty years ago, we had *plenty* of First Nations in our congregation. Boy, the church used to really hop back then, father! We had a *lot* of programs that ran both here and on the rez. There'd be cars going back and forth between here and the tribal offices multiple times per day. Until…"

Scooter paused.

"See, the thing is, father… When the Natives make a decision to do something as a group, they just go ahead and do it. They don't consult with outsiders or explain things to anyone. It happened one day that the Indians, or, a big chunk of them, decided to stop coming to services here. Archbishop Crowe was just ending his term of service as priest. He had just been elevated to the Bishop's seat. When I asked him what was going on, he said he couldn't talk about it."

Barrett made a sound of wordless puzzlement.

"The Natives began referring to the ones who stopped coming to church as 'Sasquatches.' Quiet.

Nearly invisible. Almost like they never existed. But very definitely there."

"I'll have to ask Archbishop Crowe about it," Barrett said.

"Good luck with that!" Scooter laughed. "That man can keep a secret like nobody's business."

Messiah

BARRETT LET HIMSELF INTO ST. Anne's Anglican Church, closing the main entrance softly behind him. The lights from the sanctuary spilled through the partially closed inner doors in diagonal lines on the vestibule carpet. He could sense the presence of parishioners just beyond and could hear the soft buzz of Kelly's voice. Moving stealthily, he slipped into the rear of the chapel and took a seat in the back row.

She looked beautiful up there at the front of the church. Standing before a small evening service crowd of maybe a dozen attendees, Kelly was dressed in her usual funky, haphazard fashion. The sneakers on her feet were scuffed and paint stained. The jeans she wore had a hole in one knee. She wore a sleeveless clerical shirt with the reversed collar and a seasonal stole draped around her neck. The Bible she held in her hands had a camouflage cover and was similarly worn and scuffed.

"...has been part of my ongoing pilgrimage away from my own sinfulness," she was saying. "It's always amazing to me how I usually end up drowning in sin the moment I become convinced that I know best. One of these days I'm going to get clever and recognize it as God's early warning signal that I am about to become trapped in my own BS."

Barrett sighed. Sermonizing as a kind of personal confessional had never appealed to him. But Kelly's parishioners seemed to like it. They were completely focused on her, nodding and chuckling as she spun out her homily. You could tell the congregation really loved her. So, he listened as she wound down toward the end of her remarks.

"It's only once we've reached the end of our own rope —and our own *hope*—that we come to that place where we truly are 'poor in Spirit.' And that's when God can get to work on us the way He really wants, chiseling away those parts of us that we won't need on the journey to Him. Making us aerodynamic. And better able to withstand the perilous heights of Heaven."

Barrett felt warmth bubble inside him. He had to hand it to her: Kelly knew how to get under people's skin. She was good at this. A kind of introspective spell gripped the congregation as they came forward to receive the Eucharist. Barrett hung back. She caught his eye as she was giving out the Sacrament and winked at him. He smiled back, remaining in his pew until the service ended and she had bid her flock farewell. Then she shut the church doors and came to take a seat beside him.

"So, what do you think, father?" she asked, elbowing him in the ribs playfully. "Am I ready for prime time?"

"That was a really nice homily you gave," he said. "I liked the bit about the perilous heights of Heaven."

"Yeah?" She pulled off her stole and folded it as she curled a leg under herself, her knee casually touching

Barrett's. "Well, if God made it easy it wouldn't be worthwhile, right?"

"Nothing worth having usually is," he replied.

They sat holding one another's gaze for a long moment. Then she was moving forward into his arms and they were holding one another. Quietly. Calmly. Just being together in the silence and half-light of the chapel.

"Why did you have to come into my life and start meaning so much to me so quickly?" she whispered.

"Beats me," he whispered back. He gave a final squeeze and tried to release her, but she wouldn't let go. So he laughed and let her hang onto him until she'd had enough.

"How's Officer Walton?" she asked, standing and inviting him to join her. She led him past the ultra-modern cedarwood alter installation to the back-office area of St. Anne's. He noticed a Muppets poster on her partially closed office door. She led him past it down the hallway to the kitchen.

"He's okay. No real change since you last visited him, but the medical staff is hopeful."

"And how about your friend, Gavin the cop? How's he holding up?"

"He's under a tremendous amount of stress." Barrett leaned against the counter and crossed his arms as she straightened up a mess from earlier that day. "I'm putting on my 'former cop' hat and helping out here and there. When I can."

"He's lucky to have you, Mike. This town is."

"Well...I don't know about *that*..." He chuckled. "I would prefer to think they're lucky to have you." He found her answering smirk delightful. "Sadly, I seem to be missing my deacon all of a sudden."

"Oh yeah?" She paused in tying up a trash bag to

frown, concerned at the news. "Well, do you remember where he was just before you misplaced him?"

"I think he misplaced himself." Barrett grumbled, moving to the window. "He was staying with his family on the rez. They haven't seen him, either."

"Where do you think he could be?"

"No idea." He shrugged. "How well connected are you on the rez?"

"Barely at all," she admitted. "I have one or two from the tribe who show up here, but only rarely."

"They're cautious people."

"Can you blame them?" She flapped a hand. "Given everything that's happened in the past four hundred years?"

"No."

"I'll help ya', Mike." She hefted the garbage bag and began tying the ends together. "We'll find him. For his mom's sake."

"That would be good, Kelly. Thanks."

"I'll put out the trash, then we'll go downstairs and start brainstorming. Have you eaten yet?"

"Actually, no. I'm starved."

"No worries. I just bought some really nice pasta." She hauled the bag to the door and opened it one-handed. "I'll just be a sec, here…"

Barrett felt immensely grateful for their friendship as she stepped out into the alley behind the church. He had always been one to gravitate more to male than female fellowship. This was understandable given the environments (police, the clergy) in which he had worked. But he couldn't help feeling grateful that he had become friends with this really cool woman…

And a priest, to boot. He smiled, fished his cellphone

out of his pocket, and sent a quick text to Danny Robert.

Danny, where are you?

He had just pressed SEND when a scream split the air.

For a second it froze him, all impulse to movement shocked into stillness by surprise. *Who?* He remembered Kelly was outside, heard the crashing of one garbage can tumbling into another, a shout, the sharp smack of flesh hitting flesh. Then he was shouldering open the door and hurtling into the alley.

Kelly, both hands raised, was backed against the brick wall of the church. An upended garbage can spilled trash at her feet. Someone—a figure in a black hoodie—was struggling to his feet while a second, also wearing a black hoodie, was advancing on Kelly holding a length of chain. He whipped back his arm to strike…

And Kelly moved like lightning, lips parting from her teeth in a fierce grimace, a strange fire lighting her eyes as she stepped in and swung a competent fist into the face of the one (a man, he saw) whipping the chain. Her fist connected with an audible *whop!* on the man's jaw and he shivered under the impact, grunting, the arm holding the chain drooping. Then Barrett was moving.

The second one (a woman) had just gained her feet when Barrett came up behind her, grabbed her by the belt, and the scruff of the neck and flung her head-first into the brick wall where she landed with a liquid crunch.

Chain-man was regaining his feet now, re-orienting himself and getting ready to lash out. Kelly was too far out of range to reach him before he swung, so brought up both arms to shield her head. The man drew back his arm…

And Barrett stepped up. Automatically, without even thinking about it, he went into side stance, brought his knee high and the heel of his right foot down as hard as he could into the side of the man's knee.

An audible *snap!* resounded in the alley as the man's knee broke clean. It takes only eight pounds of pressure, Barrett remembered, to break a bone and he had probably dropped close to thirty with that kick. The man's leg collapsed out from under him and he fell in any untidy heap, broken leg splayed awkwardly. Barrett noted that he did not scream.

Probably stoned out of his mind, he thought.

The woman, having recovered from her close encounter with the brick wall, was steadying herself with one hand on the church. She looked from Barrett to Kelly to the man on the ground. Then she wheeled and made for the street.

"Oh…*no* ya' don't!" Kelly strode forward and grasped the woman's hoodie in one hand and yanked. She became temporarily unbalanced, flailed against the restraint, and then managed to drag herself free. She kept two steps ahead of Kelly before reaching the street and sprinting off down the sidewalk.

"Little jackrabbit *bitch!*" Kelly panted, doubling over and placing her hands on her knees.

"What the hell happened?" Barrett went to her and immediately began scanning for injuries.

"They just came at me." Kelly shook her head. "One minute I'm out here putting the trash in the garbage can. Next thing I know, Jackrabbit and Captain Bike-chain here are going into attack mode."

"How about you?" Barrett grabbed the male attacker

by the collar and dragged him far enough off the ground to snarl directly into his face. "What's your story, huh? Huh?" He slapped the man. "Hey, don't pass out on me! *Speak*, asshole!"

The man, wobbly and unsteady from pain, managed to rally sufficiently to fix Barrett with an angry stare.

"She talked shit about the Messiah," the man managed. "Same as you!"

"What the fuck are you talking about?"

"She'll get hers," the man vowed. "And so will you!"

———

LEWIS AND AN AMBULANCE attended shortly afterwards. The Mountie stood by and took their statements as the paramedics tended to Captain Bike-chain's leg.

"Any description on the girl?" he asked.

"She was probably eighteen, nineteen," said Kelly. "Skinny. Wearing black jeans and a black hoodie."

"Aren't they all?" Lewis grunted, closing his notebook. He turned to the nearest paramedic. "What's the story?"

"His knee's broken," said the EMT. "Clean break from the side. Should heal up just fine. But he's going to need a trip to the hospital and a night or two under observation."

"Hear that?" Lewis said to the injured man. "You're getting three hots and a cot for the next few nights, courtesy of the Canadian tax-payer."

"Fuck you, cop."

"Charming!" Lewis chuckled. He turned to Barrett. "You want to press charges?"

Barrett turned to Kelly. She shook her head no.

"Are you sure, Reverend Ward?" Lewis frowned. "These two could have killed you."

"But they didn't, Sergeant Lewis," she said. "I think it will do more good in this case to practice forgiveness than bring the weight of the law to bear on them."

"That is your prerogative," Lewis said. "I'm just glad Father Barrett was here."

"Oh, he was a bit of a help." Kelly smacked his arm. "But this gal can take care of herself." She raised her fist and rubbed her bruised knuckles.

"She's ex-army," Barrett told him. "Princess Pats."

"Really?" Lewis' eyes widened. "You know your pal Mike, here, sometimes helps me out on cases. If you've got an infantry background…"

"What? You planning to put me on the SWAT team?"

Lewis laughed. "Hey, you'd probably be a big help to us! But no, that's fine. You guys go ahead and…do whatever you were planning to do. Me and the paramedics will take it from here."

"Ready for dinner, Mike?" She chucked Barrett's shoulder.

"Sounds good," he replied.

"You make a cute couple," Lewis said. And laughed again.

Solace

"YOU OKAY?"

"Yeah." She said it with a breathy sigh as she kicked off her shoes and led the way into her downstairs dwelling. "Man. If I'd only known that putting out the trash was going to become a matter of life and death…"

"This town really has gone to hell." Barrett followed her into the kitchen, where she leaned against the counter and put her head in her hands. Barrett leaned beside Kelly, lit two cigarettes and handed her one.

"Really gone to hell, huh? Thanks." She accepted the smoke, took a drag and let out a throaty chuckle through smoke. "How long have you been here?"

"Uh, coming up on a year. Give or take."

"And the town's gone to hell in a year?"

"Let's just say it's progressed further in the direction it was already heading."

"I can buy that." She pulled the soap dish from the sink and put it down beside them for ashes, then examined the ceiling, recalling the past half-hour's events. "Man, you really messed that guy up…"

"He was attacking my favorite priest."

Kelly's eyes widened. *"I'm* your favorite priest?"

"Sure are."

"Well, I'm flattered. Especially given all the role models available through your own church." She stubbed out her cigarette half-finished. "Man, I'm starving. So, I'm thinking some stuffed manicotti with Bolognese sauce. Sound good? Cool." She bent and fished a pot from the cabinet. "Could you grab me the box of pasta? Middle shelf. Cabinet by the fridge."

"Sure." Barrett located the cabinet and item in question, then hesitated as he drew down the box from the shelf. "Kelly? Uh, I think your pasta's gone bad. It's green."

"Nut!" She finished filling the pot and put it on the stove top before coming over. "It's spinach pasta. Sort of a vegan alternative to the traditional egg variety."

His face folded in disbelief. "You're vegan?" he asked.

"Well, no. I mean, yes. I mean…I'm *trying* it out."

"And my participation in this experiment is mandatory?"

Now she was laughing, moving toward him in a playfully aggressive way. "It's a good thing you became a priest, Mike," she said, grasping his arm and pretending to muscle him around. "Because you'd make an awful husband."

"Says the woman who'd make an awful wife," he countered, getting into the spirit of the thing.

"Awful wife? How *dare* you!" She stepped close to grab hold of his other arm, came chest to chest with him and paused. For a long moment they just looked at each other. Then slowly, naturally, they moved into each other's arms. Folding each other into a tight embrace, they just stood there, holding one another.

"God, you feel good," he whispered into her hair.

"I'm not in love with you," she answered. "Just halfway there."

He tightened his grip on her and she moved against him, the delicious taboo of it animating her limbs. Barrett felt it, too. She was an AA sponsor who had served him drinks. She was a priest of a denomination that contravened Biblical prohibitions against female preachers. And he had taken vows of celibacy.

She moved a little, creating some space between them. Then their foreheads were pressing together. Then...

"We shouldn't," he whispered.

"I know," she replied.

And then they were kissing.

Barrett hadn't kissed a woman in decades. So, the soft sensation of her face sliding against his own, chin bumping chin, the moist blossom of her lips encountering his, both parting and then the sweet taste and fragrance of her mouth inside his. *This! This!* This was what celibacy and the priesthood had denied him. She moaned softly into his mouth. And then his hands were rising to cup her face in his palms and her hands dropped to his belt and –

They stepped away from each other, trembling.

"Mike, I'm sorry..."

"No, Kelly. *I'm* sorry. I..."

They stared at one another, trapped. Helpless as the pot on the stove went to full boil and began belching steam up to the ceiling.

"My God." She grasped his hand. "What are we going to do?"

Barrett scanned the countertop until he spotted a bottle of Merlot. He picked it up. "How about a drink?"

Her smile held a species of relief. "Go ahead and pour us one and I'll get the pasta started. There's a corkscrew in the drawer beside the fridge."

Barrett swallowed and fought to control the trembling within himself as he dug for the corkscrew. He found wineglasses in the cupboard and poured out two drinks. Kelly accepted hers and held it aloft, a question on her face.

"Uh…" Barrett rummaged his brain for an appropriate toast. "How about to the Twelve Steps?"

"How about…to us?" She cocked her head but behind her playfulness lay a question.

Barrett tapped glasses with her.

"You know, Mike," she said, turning back to the stove. "This – what's happening between us…It's really nobody's business but ours."

"That's true." He took a sniff, then a cautious sip of the wine. It was good stuff.

"I mean…" She paused and put down her stirring spoon. "Obviously what's going on is questionable. I'm supposed to be sponsoring you in AA. You're supposed to be adhering to your vows of celibacy. *We're* supposed to be just professional colleagues. But, what's happened— what's *happening*—between us is just between us. Meaning it's nobody else's business."

He pondered this.

"I mean…even if it was a friendship. *Just* a friendship. It would still be ours. Anything we discussed would be confidential, so why wouldn't—?"

"You make an interesting point," he allowed.

"And we are, after all, only human…"

"Speak for yourself!"

They laughed and Barrett set down his wineglass. He had only taken a few sips. He studied the half-filled glass, feeling no immediate impulse to drain it. Something called him to remain here, to remain present, to remain…

With her.

He started suddenly.

My God, am I falling in love with her?

He shook his head, returning from his reverie with a grin. They busied themselves with finalizing dinner. Barrett got the sauce and bread together while Kelly finished with preparations for her weird, Martian pasta. Barrett watched her stuff the manicotti shells with cheese filling and urged himself to be open minded. They brought plates, wine bottle and glasses to the table and sat down together.

"This is the first time we've ever formally broken bread together," she said. "Guacamole notwithstanding."

"That was good," he said, drawing a napkin onto his lap. "But not a proper meal."

"We didn't even say grace."

"True." He reached out his hand with a smile. "Shall we?"

She grinned, reached out and grasped his hand. They bowed their heads.

And the phone rang.

Kelly threw her head back and roared with laughter. It was a soldier's laugh: loud, harsh and filled with undeniable good humor. Barrett found it infectious and laughed right along with her. She pushed herself up from the table and padded over to the counter where she'd left her cellphone. She picked it up and answered as she returned to her seat.

"Kelly Ward…oh!" Her eyes slid to Barrett. "Archbishop Crowe! So nice to hear from you. Yes, I… Well, yes. As a matter of fact…" She grasped Barrett's hand again. "He has been showing up for his AA meetings. More often than necessary, in fact. He... Yes. Well!"

Her eyes widened and the edges of her lips flattened in a wry smile.

"I'm honored that you would ask my opinion of Father Barrett as a priest. I think he's, well, remarkable." She squeezed his fingers. "In fact, he saved my bacon tonight."

In the ensuing silence, Barrett could make out the buzz of Crowe's voice across the digital connection.

"Father Barrett intervened in an attack against me," she continued. "I had just finished evening services when I was attacked by two street people, one of whom came at me swinging a chain. If it wasn't for Father Barrett, I would have wound up dead. He's here right now, as a matter of fact."

She flicked a grin at Barrett.

"Of course, you can speak to him. Here." She handed over the phone.

"Your excellency," Barrett said, accepting the cell. "What a surprise."

"Father Barrett. Mike!" Crowe sounded relieved. "Are you alright? Reverend Ward was just telling me about the attack at St. Anne's."

"I'm okay, thanks." Barrett stopped short of calling him by his first name in front of Kelly. "Kelly is okay following the attack and so am I. I was forced to, ah, use a little bit of coercive correction... All in the Lord's name, of course."

"Meaning you beat somebody up again?" Crowe sighed. "Father Barrett, if you'll recall, not long after you arrived in Fulton, you were arrested for beating up a man in a bar—"

"He was in the midst of assaulting a woman, your excellency."

"True." Crowe paused. "Same thing here, I take it. Reverend Ward was unharmed."

"Yes. Same thing here, your excellency. She's quite… intact." Barrett flashed a smile at Kelly and squeezed her fingers.

"Well…" Crowe chuckled. "It sounds to me like the relationship between the two of you is working out to your mutual benefit. And for that I am prayerfully grateful. I think putting the two of you together may turn out to be one of my better ideas."

"I, uh, would tend to agree, your excellency." Beneath the table, Barrett bumped her knee with his own and Kelly chuckled.

"This is actually a good opportunity for me to broach another topic." Crowe paused. "I just got off the phone with Danny Robert's family. They're very concerned. Apparently, there's still no sign of him."

"I haven't come across him either, archbishop."

"Go pay them a visit, would you?" Crowe's grave concern was evident even across the connection. "Gather what information you can. Let them know Mother Church takes his absence very seriously. Put on your old Papal investigator cap."

"I will, your excellency." Barrett signaled his concern to Kelly with a motion of his head.

"Find him for me, Mike. I'm counting on you."

———

BARRETT SAT BACK and pondered the phone for a moment before handing it back to Kelly.

"Everything okay?" she asked.

He shook his head. "It's Danny Robert. His excellency received a call from the family. He's still missing. He's asked me to look into it further."

"Oh, yeah?" She toyed with her wineglass. "Didn't you used to do investigations for the church?"

"Yeah. For the Curia. It's, uh, how I ended up here, actually…"

"What sorts of things? Did you investigate, I mean…"

"It was for the Congregation of the Doctrine of the Faith. That's what they call the Inquisition these days." He picked up his wine glass, raised it to his lips and then set it down untouched. He suddenly didn't feel like having a drink. "I dealt with a lot of professional misconduct. Including, uh…"

She waited.

"Including…priestly sexual misconduct." The irony of that statement in light of their present predicament stung uncomfortably. "It kind of pushed me to the edge, and… Well, let's just say some 'professional re-evaluation' was called for. And I ended up here."

"Interesting." Her smirk was back. "I'm thinking there's a story there that's worth teasing out. But probably not tonight."

"Yeah. Crowe wants me to go talk to Danny Robert's family. Tonight." He checked his watch. "Right now."

She remained perfectly still. For a moment Barrett imagined disappointment—possibly even anger—in her eyes. But then she surprised him by rising and grabbing her jacket.

"C'mon," she said. "I'll go with you. Let's go."

Lore

THEY TOOK Barrett's parish Hyundai and drove out through the gathering dark across the silent streets of town. They followed the main road out toward Crowley Street which demarcated the northern boundary of Fulton—a DMZ of strip joints, greasy spoons and oil-pit garages. They passed the Avro Lane trailer park, then the trucking companies and darkened lumber yard with its forbidding mountains of finished timber stacked into the sky. Shortly beyond lay the access road and signage marking the boundaries of the reserve.

As was ever the case when crossing into this section of the landscape, Barrett noticed changes in road maintenance and infrastructure. The macadam was worn here, strewn with potholes, and the signage was worn and bent. Untrimmed trees loomed over the road and the sagging roofs of government subsidized housing loomed out between overgrown yards, some piled with junk and discarded furniture. All the accoutrements of First Nations rural poverty were on display.

"Mike, when you came here, did your church

provide you with any sort of in-services or training about how to interact with the local First Nati— Why are you laughing?"

"Because not long after getting here I received an 'in-service' courtesy of the local rez punk bicycle gang."

"Oh?"

"Yeah. They waylaid and punched the shit out of me on the way back from the liquor store one day." Barrett sniffed. "Stole my box of wine, too, the little shit-weasels."

"My *God*, Barrett! You're bitter."

"I suppose so." He scratched his cheek. "Either that or I'm just a realist. I mean, take a look around here." He waved a hand at the lights in the windows of the sagging houses around them. "Centuries of colonization, apathy, abandonment, and neglect. What has Christianity ever done for these people except enslave them? Sure! You have the odd individual here and there who professes and loves everything about the faith. But for the most part, the church's legacy with these people has been a failure."

"Maybe we can make it up to them."

"That could take a long, long time."

They kept an eye on the house numbers until finding the one they were looking for. He pulled into the driveway of the single-story house owned by Danny Robert's family. Two windows dominated the façade, one dark and the other lit. Absent curtains, the window looked into a lit living room. Barrett recognized a familiar ballcap and pair of glasses.

"The Chief's here." He braked to a halt and switched off the Hyundai. "That's a good thing. He's got a mind for people and faces. Knows every single person on this reserve by first name and can tell you where half of them were and what they were doing yesterday afternoon."

"Nice." Kelly slipped out the passenger side and shut her door, following him up the path to the porch. "You seem to have developed a good relationship with the man."

As if by magic, the door opened on Barrett's approach. Although a middle-aged woman held it, it was the Chief standing behind her who was obviously the official greeter. He smiled and nodded at Barrett, then extended a hand to Kelly.

"You must be Reverend Ward," he said. "We haven't met. Welcome to our ancestral lands. I'm the tribal chief, here."

"Your honor," she said quietly and Barrett admired the cool way she did it.

"Do you know Danny's sister?" The Chief turned to the woman holding the door. "Connie, say hello to Father Barrett."

"Hi." Barrett extended a hand. "We spoke the other night. I've come to follow up on Danny."

Connie stood looking at Barrett's hand awkwardly. A long moment passed and he dropped it back by his side. He and Kelly exchanged a look. In addition to the Chief and Connie, there seemed to be another visitor in the place – a brooding presence in the living room. Without even having to say a word, the Chief ushered them through. From the way he and Connie stood back from a blue couch by the far wall, Barrett could tell that was where they wanted them to sit. So, they moved in and sat down, waiting for everyone else to arrange themselves. In the interim, Barrett studied the final houseguest.

She was an aged woman—an Elder in First Nations

parlance. But her exact age, given her heritage and coloring, was impossible to guess with any precision. She could have been sixty. She could have been eighty. But she was a broad-faced, thick-boned woman with muscle across the shoulder and extra weight to throw around. And her black eyes darted quickly, possessively, from person to person in the room before settling on Barrett with a kind of cruel flatness.

"Father Barrett, Reverend Ward," said the Chief. "This is Louise Joe. She's Danny's and Connie's grandmother. Louise, these two are the Catholic and Anglican priests in town these days."

Louise Joe's eyes flicked from Barrett to Kelly and back again. Without looking at Kelly, she said, "I like your tattoos."

To Barrett she said nothing. Just stared.

"Um, thanks. We're very concerned about Danny," Kelly said. Given the temperature in the room, Barrett let her take the lead. "Mike here hasn't seen him and neither have you guys. So we came to begin our own search."

"How long have you been in town, honey?" asked Louise Joe mildly.

"About four months now," said Kelly. "Not very long at all."

"And what about you?" Louise Joe asked Barrett. "You've been around for a while. Long enough to get a reputation. They say you're a violent man. And a drinker. That true?"

"I like a drink now and then," Barrett affirmed. "And I never start fights. But I finish them. Particularly if someone strong is abusing someone weak. I never allow that to stand."

Something about the way she examined him after he

said this unsettled Barrett. There was a hurt frankness there—the look of someone who had been well and truly betrayed in her life. From her expression, Barrett might have guessed that she somehow held him personally responsible for these betrayals. He reminded himself that he was in uniform, as he had been back in his days as a cop. How many times had he interacted with some civilian who considered him the root of the world's evil simply because he wore a badge?

People harbor similar feelings about the church, he thought.

"Yes, we're all very worried about Danny," said the Chief in the ensuing silence. "We're trying to figure out what might have happened to him. Father, when was the last time you spoke to him?"

"It was yesterday, when I was on my way back from a meeting with Archbishop Crowe—"

At the mention of Crowe's name, Louise Joe turned and spoke to the Chief in their native tongue. It was a short statement, just a few words long, but it caused the Chief to nod.

"I pulled over on the road to speak to him. He was just calling to check in and update me on a few things." Barrett remembered Crowe's injunction to keep Archbishop Radcliffe's presence in town low-key so did not mention him. "We talked, made arrangements to touch base in the next day or so and then hung up."

"Do you remember anything from the phone call?" Kelly asked. "Like, anything you said or he said that might have triggered him?"

"No." Barrett spread his hands. "It was all very routine. The sort of talk we'd had a dozen times before." He turned to Connie. "I spoke to you a while later. You mentioned he hadn't come home. Was he a creature of routine?"

"He always came home at the same time every night," said Louise Joe, answering for Connie. "A lot of young men aren't like that, but Danny liked to keep a routine. Always hung his coat on the same peg. Always put his shoes in the same place. He never changed. So when it got be an hour past when he usually came home, we knew. And Connie called you." She cocked her head and asked: "How is Father Crowe these days?"

"He's an archbishop now," Barrett said. "He likes Danny very much. We all do. He's going to be a very successful priest."

"We're very proud of him," affirmed the Chief. "He really turned his life around from when he was young, running about and getting into trouble. Perhaps because of him, more people from the reserve here will start going back to church."

"I thought the Archbishop was Radcliffe," Louise Joe was saying. "That was who was Archbishop back in the day. Back when Father Crowe was running the Catholic church here in town."

"Archbishop Radcliffe is retired," Barrett told her and left it at that.

Louise Joe absorbed this in silence, shifting her bulk in the chair and brushing imaginary crumbs from the front of her dress. It was an interesting gesture because Louise Joe's movements and facial expressions were precise. She was not the sort to drop crumbs on herself while eating. But he supposed the brushing motions, like her lack of facial expressions, were intended to achieve tactical ends. They certainly succeeded in getting everyone's attention.

"I remember the days of Archbishop Radcliffe," she

said quietly when she was again still. "This was years ago. Back when my Gordon was still alive." She drew in a sudden breath – almost a gasp. But it was quiet. "Things were different then. This was back in the Seventies, Eighties." She looked at Connie. "You ask the Chief and he'll tell you. Things were harder then. Less money from the government. Pierre Trudeau never gave a shit about us."

"Gordon was a very hard worker," said the Chief quietly, and Barrett couldn't get over the sensation that this conversation was being held specifically for his benefit.

"Does that surprise you? That my husband would work hard?" The flat, cruel stare was back as Louise Joe's eyes dropped on him again. "He worked road crew. He'd rake gravel, ride the steam roller, hold the stop sign on rainy days in the middle of all that traffic. I used to worry for him. But he told me, *Louise, we're going to get ahead.*"

"Gordon thought about money an awful lot," said the Chief quietly.

"We were going to get ahead." Louise Joe's voice suddenly softened in a tone of nostalgia. "He wanted to get enough money together to open a sporting goods store here on the rez. It was a *good* idea. A lot of Indian people hunt and fish and having a good store here would bring trade from the town and from white tourists."

The pause after this statement was like swimming into a cold patch in a warm lake on a summer day. There was a sense of forbidding depth, of something dark lurking down there. Barrett could guess from her words that the store had never opened. What he did not know was why.

"He died soon after that day at your church," Louise

Joe told Barrett. "That day we came to find out what had become of our money and he broke the window. We stopped going to church that day. A lot of us did."

Barrett began to ask a question, but the Chief interrupted him.

"Find Danny for us, father," he said, a grim authority weighting his words. "He's very precious to us and we want him back."

———

HE PULLED up and parked in front of Kelly's church. She grappled him to her, hung on hard, and bit his ear.

"You keep me in the loop, padre," she whispered.

"Yep." He kissed her neck, half-released/half-flung her away from him. She shoved his chest hard, smirked and got out of the car.

He drove home, suddenly craving a drink. The dark streets crept by until he pulled into the driveway of the rectory. A single light shone from his basement office window. Curious, he went down.

Miss Dolan must have released Radcliffe from his room at some point during the day because he was sitting at Barrett's desk, pounding away on the keyboard of his desktop computer. The old dot matrix printer spat out sheet after sheet of closely spaced text. There was already a pile of print-out stacked high on the desk.

"Your excellency." Barrett blinked. "Uh, nice to see you. Listen, I just want to check my e-mail—"

Radcliffe hunched forward, intent on his typing, and let out a low growl.

"Okay." Barrett held up his hands. "No problem. I'll do it tomorrow."

Burn

IF HE WAS GOING to keep Radcliffe locked in the guest room, it was obvious Barrett would need a replacement lock. *Somehow Miss Dolan figured out the combination,* he thought angrily. Fortunately, the next morning was a shopping day which meant she wouldn't arrive until later. This meant he had some time.

Barrett dressed in his bedroom. Then, shoes in hand, he snuck down the hallway in his stocking feet to the guest room and peered inside. Radcliffe lay sprawled across the bed, snoring heavily, a trio of empty beer bottles on the table beside him. Barrett eased the door shut and then set the hasp over the lock ring. Then, picking up the combination lock where Miss Dolan had left it on a hallway table, he dropped it into his pocket, went downstairs to the kitchen and put on his shoes.

It was only 8:30 AM according to the Hyundai's dashboard clock. The streets were deserted at this hour. Most people, it seemed, couldn't be bothered to stir themselves from home prior to 10. Fortunately, McLellan's Big Box Retail kept corporate hours, opening at 7 and closing at 11, just like the Walmart in Campbell River. He would dash in, get what he needed, and be back before anyone even knew he was up.

He didn't connect the plume of smoke rising skyward with McLellan's until he pulled into the parking area. The vast lot was empty aside from a few cars belonging to staff and customers by the side entrance. His concern grew as he approached the store, and the shouting he heard upon stepping inside confirmed that something was up. A female greeter stared, slack-mouthed, as two male employees ran up the main aisle toward the back of the store.

"What's going on?" Barrett asked.

"Not sure," she replied. "I think somebody tried to steal—"

That was as far as she got before Barrett was running full tilt after the employees. His foot strikes echoed through the mostly empty big box and his sprinting form drew surprised glances from puzzled clerks as he hurtled down the main aisle toward an open fire door, the sound of its alarm piercing the morning quiet.

"Father Barrett!"

He turned. Homer Anderson, the store detective and a parishioner, met Barrett where two aisles intersected. Both skidded to a stop.

"Homer! What's going on?"

"We got two ballers, father! Roughed up an employee and went out the fire door!"

"Let's get 'em!"

They ran. Sitting on the ground by the fire door was an elderly female employee. She held a bloody bandage to her face as a second clerk, a young Sikh man, knelt beside her administering First Aid. Homer skidded to a stop and pulled out a cell phone.

"Amir? You got this? Need an ambulance?"

"We're okay, Homer," replied the Sikh clerk. "But Stan and Roger went out after them!"

Barrett and Homer needed no more prompting. They barreled out through the open fire door to a scene straight out of hell.

Thirty feet behind the building, gouts of black smoke and flame erupted from a dumpster. Two employees dressed in McLellan's sales vests were engaged in a hand-to-hand melee with three people. One was attempting to wrest a full hockey bag away from a man dressed in black jeans and a hoodie. Another hoodie was trying to extricate his bicycle from behind the burning dumpster while warding off blows from the second employee. The third assailant, a woman, was dragging something from her pocket…

"Stan!" screamed Homer. "Look out!"

The man attempting to wrest the hockey bag from the thief turned just in time to avoid a blow from the woman's ASP baton. The female thief had the titanium rod fully extended and was whipping the weighted tip back and forth. As Barrett watched, Homer put his head down and shoulder-charged the woman, slamming her up against the dumpster. She hit the side with a grunt, dropped the ASP baton, and began grappling with the store detective.

Meanwhile, the one with the bike had managed to grab the hockey bag, shoulder it, and begin peddling down the path that led into the woods behind the store. Roger, the other clerk, lunged at him but got knocked off course when the second thief body-checked him to the ground. Then the thief on the bike and his friend took off down the path, disappearing into the forest. The whine of a police siren split the morning.

Barrett went to back up Homer. The store detective was down on one knee, securing handcuffs to the squirming, spitting woman he had brought face-down onto the cement scant meters from the burning dumpster.

"Get her cuffed up and let's move her," Barrett said, shielding his eyes against the smoke and heat. He saw Gavin Lewis swerve into the lot in his Crown Vic, followed closely by a pump truck from the Fulton volunteer fire department. Barrett leaned down and grasped the woman by her left arm and lifted as Homer did the same on her right side. Lewis, meanwhile, had pulled aside to permit the pump engine access to the dumpster before parking the Crown Vic crosswise in the alley to block traffic.

"What have we got here?" he asked, rolling out of the driver side door and squinting at the struggling woman Barrett and Homer held between them. "Shoplifter? Arsonist? Or both?"

"Both, sergeant," puffed Homer. "Three of them went out the fire door and set the dumpster alight to cover their escape. We've also got two others that made it away with probably about $600 worth of merchandise."

"Put her in the back." Lewis held open the rear door for them.

"Aren't you gonna read me my rights, pig?" spat the girl. "You have to read me my Miranda Rights."

"That's 'sergeant' to you. And you watch too much TV. We're in Canada, sweetheart," said Lewis in a sugary tone. "It's called being Chartered up here. Now sit down, shut the fuck up, and I'll be right with you." He slammed the door and turned to Homer. "Homer, do me a favor, would you? Go ahead and grab her a bottle of drinking water…"

"I'll get it," said Barrett, laying a hand on Homer's arm. "Homer, why don't you stay out here and brief Gavin?"

"Will do, father. Thanks."

Barrett went into the store, grabbed a bottle of water from a shelf, and explained to a clerk what was going on. The clerk nodded, told him to take it, and made a note for himself to write it off from inventory. When Barrett returned outside, the flames from the dumpster had been extinguished. A mushroom cloud of pale grey smoke was dissipating beneath the firemen's hoses. Lewis had opened the back door of the Crown Vic to allow their suspect some air. Gavin, meanwhile, was standing a few feet off with Homer, getting the details of the situation.

"...came in around half-an-hour ago. Separately, but it was obvious they were working together. I mean...they all *dress* alike." Homer flapped a hand at the open door. "They might as well be wearing uniforms. Anyway, she stole the hockey bag and passed it off to the other two guys, who proceeded to fill it up. Like I said, a couple hundred dollars' worth of merchandise."

"You have CCTV footage?" Lewis was asking.

"Yeah. I did the entire surveillance on CCTV."

Barrett leaned into the rear of the Crown Vic. "I brought you some water," he told the girl, shaking the bottle. "Care for some?"

She was a thin-faced gamine—the sort who would be pretty if she washed and donned a change of clothes. But from the curl of her lip and the hard-eyed stare she threw Barrett's way it was obvious she'd been on the streets long enough to absorb its harshest lessons and adapt accordingly. In response to Barrett's question, she turned slightly in his direction and lifted her chin. Barrett opened the bottle of water. She sat forward, adjusting the position of the wrists behind her back. Barrett held the water to her lips.

She took two quick gulps and a third which filled her cheeks. Then she yanked her head away and spat the water in Barrett's face.

"Okay." Barrett capped the water bottle and brushed droplets from his cassock. "I guess you've had your fill. What's your name, honey?"

"Die, priest pig!"

"Charming. Named after mom, were you?"

"Asshole! Kid fucker!"

Barrett sighed and stepped over to Homer and Lewis.

"She's a real nice girl," he said. "Warm. Friendly. Excellent manners."

"She's a fucking meth-head," Lewis grumbled. "Homer, can you get me the footage and a Report to Crown Counsel?"

"Sure thing, sergeant. I'll have it for you this afternoon."

"Great. Just drop it off through the mail slot at the office." He clapped a hand on Barrett's shoulder. "Now let's go have another word with our new friend."

The fire department was just finishing up, closing down their hoses as an oily, grey oval of water pooled under the dumpster. Homer side-stepped this as he entered the fire door, pulling it shut behind him. Barrett followed Lewis to the Crown Vic. Reaching in, he took the girl by the elbow and, none too gently, drew her from the car and stood her up against the side as he unceremoniously began going through her pockets.

"Anything in here gonna stick me?" he asked. "Any knives, needles, sharps?"

"Fuck you, pig."

"I'll take that as a no." His fist came out of one

pocket and opened over the trunk. A bus transfer, a twist of tin foil, some coins, and a hard candy in a clear wrapper dropped onto the car. "You one of the Garbage Messiah's kids?"

"Your days are coming to an end, pig man! The Messiah's the fucking *king!*" she snapped.

"King of what?" Lewis snapped back. "Of Shit Hill? Jesus!" He spun her around, shoved her into the back of the Crown Vic, and slammed the door. Then he turned, leaned against the car, and rubbed his eyes. "Those two that got away are probably at the Dump right now. Walton's still out of commission, so I've asked Campbell River to send over a couple of units. We'll head up there tonight for a look around. Any luck finding your missing deacon?"

"Not yet," Barrett said. "Had a meeting last night with his family…"

"Was old Louise Joe there?" Lewis grinned.

"Yeah. She talked about her late husband. About dreams they had of opening a store."

"I remember." Lewis nodded. "Gordon actually came and talked to me about it. He was saving up his money to open a hunting and fishing store on the rez. Damned good idea, if you ask me. But it never went anywhere."

"Gavin, what was the problem between them and Archbishop Crowe when he was parish priest here?"

"Like I said…it was years ago." He shrugged. "Had something to do with money. That's all I know. Why? Should I get the file sent up from archives?"

Barrett paused, considering this at length.

"It might be worth doing, Gavin. If you can make the time."

"No problem, padre. It's just a phone call. I'll make it tonight."

First In The Field

"WELL, FATHER!" Miss Dolan flashed Barrett a chilly smile as he entered the kitchen and laid the bag containing the new lock he'd bought on the kitchen table. "As you probably noticed, Archbishop Radcliffe is absolutely fine and of no danger to himself or anyone else. I let him out of his room yesterday."

"I noticed." Barrett marched to the kitchen sink, reached up and pulled down the box of wine from the cupboard above the basin. "Thank you for that."

"You're most welcome, father. As your housekeeper, it's my obligation to attend to the well-being of you and your guests." She smiled, either ignoring or oblivious to his sarcasm. "I trust he didn't cause any damage or bother."

"Aside from monopolizing my computer and refusing to let me check my e-mail, no."

"Oh, Archbishop Radcliffe was most insistent! Said he absolutely *must* have access to a computer so he could write something very important!"

"I see." Barrett poured some wine into his mug,

finished half and topped it up before resuming. "Well, that's very thoughtful of you. Providing the archbishop access to my computer. And my printer. And ink, paper, and toner..."

"Oh, no need to thank me, father."

"No, really. Your generosity with my stuff is...well, epic." He sipped wine and made for the basement stairs. "I'll be in my office."

Miss Dolan said something indistinct as he began clattering down the basement steps but he didn't care enough to turn around and ask her to repeat herself. He had had enough of Miss Dolan for one morning. He longed for the safety and isolation of his office, its closed door and Wi-Fi connection to the monochromatic, predictable world of the internet.

He reached the bottom of the steps, switched his mug to his left hand and opened the door.

The room was a shambles. Books had been pulled down from their shelves, opened and left scattered across every available surface. Half-filled cups and empty beer bottles took up the remainder of the table and desk space. Empty food containers were strewn across the rug. Sitting hunched over the computer, Archbishop Radcliffe pounded furiously on the keyboard. The stack of papers by the printer had grown considerably.

"Good morning, your excellency."

Radcliffe ignored him and kept typing.

"I see you're still working on your...project. Is there any chance I could check my e-mail?"

"Ha!"

"Okay." Barrett smiled tightly and stepped out, easing the door shut behind him.

Miss Dolan was upstairs. And Radcliffe had monopolized his office.

Damn!

Barrett sighed and wandered into the rear portion of the basement, where the hot water heater yammered and belched its bellicose anthem. He took a seat on a stack of cinderblocks, took one last sip of wine then called Archbishop Crowe's number in Vancouver.

"Archbishop Crowe's office. Brother Steven speaking."

"Hi." Barrett was surprised to reach Crowe's assistant, the patient and ever-hovering Brother Steven. "This is Mike Barrett in Fulton calling for the archbishop."

"Father Barrett, hello. Nice to hear you. Unfortunately, Archbishop Crowe is out of the office at the moment. In fact, he's on his way to Vancouver Island now."

"Really? Okay. Any idea when he'll be back?"

"I suspect he'll be in touch with you, father. The archbishop has a number of stops to make, mostly in Victoria and Nanaimo. But I know Fulton is on the itinerary."

"I see. Okay. Well, it's good to know that we're in the archbishop's thoughts."

"Always. Shall I take a message?"

"Just please let him know I called. Thanks."

Barrett hung up, finished his wine and left his empty mug on the tool bench. He needed refuge from the day's insanity. So he exited via the basement door, pulled out car keys and got into the Hyundai.

HIS PREFERRED WATERING hole was the Junction. A dive bar with a cement floor and the ever-present odor of bleach and human despair, the place served as an unofficial meeting place for himself and Lewis whenever they were off duty. At this time of the day, it was empty. Barrett let himself in and wandered past the pool table, juke box and framed posters of James Dean and Elvis to take a seat at the bar. The barkeep wandered over and dropped a cardboard coaster in front of him.

"I'll have a beer, please," he said. "Anything new these days?"

"Not much, father," said the barman, grabbing a glass to pull a pint of Lucky. "But I guess it's my day for the religious crowd."

"How so?"

Just then the door to the women's bathroom opened and Kelly appeared. She grinned at Barrett, made a beeline for him and chucked him on the shoulder before taking the stool next to his.

"Make it a pitcher," she said. "On me." She put her credit card on the bar, collected the pitcher and glasses when they arrived, and tilted her head toward a table. "Let's grab a little privacy, Father Barrett. No offense," she said to the bartender. "We have super-secret priest stuff to discuss."

"Sure thing." The bartender smiled and began polishing glasses.

"Fancy meeting you here," Kelly snickered, pouring them drinks once they sat down in a booth. "If I didn't know better, I'd say your efforts to achieve sobriety have shipwrecked on the rocks."

"Given the morning I've just had, I'd say yeah. Total shipwreck." Barrett drained half his beer glass at a go. "I got pulled into an arrest at McLellan's. Homer Anderson, the LP there…"

"LP?"

"Loss prevention officer. Anyway, he's a parishioner

of mine and a friend. He had a violent arrest underway when I arrived. Three homeless who'd ducked out through an emergency door and set fire to the dumpster to cover their tracks…"

"Set fire to a *dumpster?*"

"You'd be amazed the things people will do to avoid arrest. Including putting innocent lives in danger." He studied the bubbles rising from the bottom of his glass. "You've had your own run-in with the criminals marauding through Fulton these days. It's getting progressively more violent."

"Hasn't it always been?"

"Not like this." He shook his head. "A janitor assaulted at the community center. A girl knifed during a break-in at my church. Walton shot. You attacked outside your parish. Now this fire…"

"And it's all tied to the group that lives on that hill?"

"The Dump. Yeah."

"Yeah. I have something to say about that. But before I do. This Garbage Messiah." Kelly narrowed her eyes. "That guy in the alley screamed something about him. And you mentioned something about him being tied to all these crimes."

"It's just a suspicion we have. But it's a strong one." Barrett hunched forward, placing his elbows on the table and ordering his thoughts carefully. "*He* keeps getting mentioned by perps and victims. But he's never around. And the violence really took a quantum leap right after he showed up in town a few months ago. You know who I keep thinking about?"

"Who?"

"Charles Manson." Barrett held up a hand. "I know it sounds crazy but hear me out. Those awful murders in California back in the Sixties. He wasn't there but the murders were committed by people that were close to him. The prosecution proved that he somehow managed to influence his followers to do them in order to ignite a race war."

"Helter Skelter. The whole Beatles song thing."

"Yeah. What if the Garbage Messiah is like Manson? What if he has some power, some sway over the people around him at the Dump? What if he's ordering them to do all these violent crimes? What if...?" Barrett held up a finger. "What if he has some plan he's working on? Some goal he's working toward? What if—"

"Mike. I think I might have seen your deacon out at the Dump."

————

BARRETT WAS SO TAKEN by surprise by this that he fell completely silent. Then Kelly was speaking.

Of course, she had no idea what Danny Robert looked like. And it had only been from a distance, and that briefly. But her duties of the morning had caused her to be out and about in her Bug. She had collapsed household chores (shopping) in with parish duties (visiting sick parishioners) and a brief excursion (to the nearby woods) for some bird watching.

"Yes. I birdwatch. Wipe that look off your face, Barrett."

"Sorry."

On her way to the woods, she decided to check out the north end of town – an area of Fulton she rarely visited. A spirit of exploration had inspired her to take a detour and she'd found herself on the rise overlooking the hill where the town homeless had taken to gathering.

Out of curiosity, she'd pulled out her birdwatching binoculars and scanned the camp.

Everything she had seen tallied with Barrett's comparison of the Garbage Messiah to Charles Manson. She described the homeless camp in some detail. Apparently, things there were a lot more organized than expected. It seemed there were a great many homeless present during her period of observation – more than she had anticipated.

"What did Sergeant Lewis say about the number of homeless in the town?" she asked.

"That it's increased. Noticeably."

"I saw maybe two or three dozen."

"*That* many?" Barrett was surprised.

But it seemed that her figures were bang on. As Kelly continued her narration of events, Barrett grew ever more uncomfortable.

The 'Messiah' appeared to have convened some sort of meeting. The Dump's denizens had gathered, emerging from their tents and lean-tos to sit cross-legged in a trio of concentric circles on the ground. The Messiah had stepped into the center and begun speaking. He went on, she claimed, for some length of time. But it was what happened at the end that shocked her.

After speaking for perhaps fifteen minutes, the Messiah paused and waved his hand. Two men emerged from a tent holding the arms of a girl. At the Messiah's orders, they brought her to the center of the circle and pushed her down on her knees.

"The Messiah had her roll up her sleeve," Kelly said. "Then he took out a knife and cut a diagonal slash across her forearm. It must have hurt because she cried out loud enough for me to hear, even at a distance. But it was obviously intended as some sort of punishment or disciplinary action. Because when he was done, the people sitting on the ground applauded. Then he dismissed them."

———

BARRETT SAT motionless for a long time after she was finished.

"So where did Danny Robert come into all this?"

"I'm not *sure* it was him," she qualified. "But when everybody scattered, a young First Nations man who had been standing quietly in the rear came out. He had a First Aid kit with him. He went to the girl that had been cut, knelt down and began tending to her. There was just something about him, Mike. He had that priestly vibe – you know the one. That 'I-was-in-seminary' gravitas that we priests carry around. I'm not a hundred percent sure, but…"

"No, it sounds like him." Barrett examined the ceiling. Lewis had mentioned Danny Robert running with a rough crowd in his youth. Was it possible some of the homeless were old friends of his? It seemed likely.

"Lewis is planning to raid the Dump with reinforcements from Campbell River some time tonight." He checked his watch. "We could get there first. Take a look around."

"Mike, they threatened to kill us for 'dissing' the Messiah."

"So we go armed." He narrowed his eyes. "I have a piece. I'll bring it. We'll go. Show them we're not afraid. You got the stones to back me up, lady?"

"Just say when and where and I'll have your back." She toasted him. "Dirty Princess Pat, here. First in the field."

Vow

"YOU REALIZE HOW DANGEROUS THIS IS..."

"Anything worth accomplishing usually is."

"*Ooooo*...kay." Kelly jiggled her car keys and laughed. "All aboard the Garbage Messiah Express."

Barrett slid into the passenger seat of Kelly's aerodynamic VW Bug. From the outside it resembled a spaceship but the interior reflected the messy and hectic life of a working pastor. Food wrappers and empty cardboard coffee cups were strewn across the dash. Every cup holder and cubby was crowded with pens, eyeglass cases, packs of chewing gum. Kelly's knapsack sat upright in the back seat, its zip undone, the edge of her laptop visible poking up from inside. Sarah McLachlan warbled movingly mid-song as Kelly spun the ignition.

"Sorry," she muttered, dimming the volume on the CD player.

"Sarah McLachlan, huh?" He lifted a jewel CD case from the cubby beneath the stereo. "I'd have thought she's a little too crunchy and granola-girl for an ex-soldier like you."

"Oh, yeah?" She snatched the CD case from his fingers. "What do you listen to? No, wait. Let me guess. You strike me as a Merle Haggard kind of guy."

"Who?"

"Never mind." She shifted the gears and coasted out of her church's driveway and onto the main road, steering toward town.

It was an hour past sundown and the streets were quiet and deserted. Lights burned in the windows of shop fronts on main street and Barrett could see Lewis was at work in the RCMP office, probably waiting for the backup he'd requested earlier from Campbell River. Still no sign of them, which was fine by Barrett. He wanted a crack at the Garbage Messiah and his crew alone before the horsemen came to queer the pitch.

Barrett guided Kelly to the street that ran above the hilltop site of the Dump. As she pulled over and parked, Barrett could see from a distance someone had built a fire in the homeless camp. The shapes of the Garbage Messiah's tribesmen and -women were visible silhouetted against its flames.

"Still got your birdy glasses?"

"Glove compartment."

Barrett rummaged among the collection of maps and auto insurance papers until he found the miniature set of binoculars. He drew them out and lifted them to his face. Although small, their magnification power was intense. The faces and details of those sitting around the fire jumped into sharp focus. Barrett recognized one of the assailants from the attack behind St. Anne's. She, like the rest, were hunched forward, paying attention to a figure who stood slightly apart from the crowd.

It was him, the Garbage Messiah. Barrett felt an instinctive clutch of revulsion watching the thin, bearded figure hold forth in dramatic fashion. His long, slender limbs flailed and his eyes glimmered with dark fire as he lectured his true believers, holding them spellbound with his bullshit theatrics. Barrett flashed on images of Hitler, Manson, Mussolini. But the one image that settled and made him grind his teeth was Rasputin.

"You strapped?" Kelly took the binoculars from him, glassed the camp, and then replaced them in the glove box.

"Yep." Barrett reached around for the concealed holster at the small of his back and withdrew the slim black Glock 19. He checked it over.

"Can I see?"

"Sure." Barrett handed over the weapon butt first. Kelly accepted it, ejected the magazine, racked the slide, and gave the pistol a thoroughly professional once over. She replaced the magazine, thumbed the slide closed and paused, gazing down at the weapon's profile.

"What's this?" Her finger traced the engraving near the barrel's snout.

"Those are the Papal coat-of-arms." Barrett took the back the Glock and examined the glyph. "Any weapon registered to the Swiss Guard and kept in their armory bears the Papal arms. Those few Vatican investigators who actually carry weapons draw them from the armory. The etching ensures the weapons can never be resold."

Kelly flattened her lips and nodded slowly. "Cool."

"As cool as a dirty Princess Pat?"

"No. Nothing is that cool."

He grinned. "We gonna do this?"

"What's the plan?"

"I want you to take the lead," Barrett said. "You be the 'front' man and I'll be right behind you. If you do the talking, that way I can watch the perimeter and deal with any trouble."

"Sounds like a plan." She smiled. "Let's roll."

———————

THEY LEFT the car and began walking, hiking to the main road and following it down toward the Dump. This area of town was not usually frequented by the public. There was nothing out here – no stores, no gas stations, just an empty stretch of street between the industrial zone and the onramps to the highway. He and Kelly fell into an easy rhythm, matching each other stride for stride.

"This bring back memories of marches?" he asked.

"Jesus, did we ever march. Miles at a time. Wear the calluses right off your feet." She cocked her head and asked, "What about you, copper? Do the boys in blue ever march?"

"Sure. In training. Marching up and down the goddam parade square. Useless activity."

"What's the longest march you've ever been on?"

"Oh, I dunno." He frowned, remembering. "Maybe an hour or two?"

She laughed. "Pussy!"

"Well how about you, Princess Dirty Boots?"

"Ever hear of Hyena Road?"

"Can't say I have."

"In Kandahar. It's the most godforsaken stretch of real estate on the planet. We did a ten-hour forced march down it, dodging snipers and IEDs all the way."

Barrett considered this. The Canadian Armed Forces had seen and done terrible things in Afghanistan. Which meant that if she had been there, she would have experienced her fair share of horrors. He suddenly felt the unfamiliar sensation of pity for her.

"Does it haunt you?" he asked gently.

For a long moment, Kelly didn't answer. But when she did, her voice was toneless and husky:

"Yeah."

Barrett wrapped an arm around her shoulder, squeezing her to him and then letting go.

————

THE HOMELESS ENCAMPMENT was close now. They could see the glow of the fire from the base of the hill and hear snatches of the Garbage Messiah's voice as he ranted. Bits of individual words occasionally blew down from the summit but it was mostly a buzz of white noise – the background static of his garbage kingdom.

"If things get hairy, get behind me. Fast." Barrett's hand strayed to the Glock in its back holster. "I'll draw and cover our retreat."

"Roger that. I expect resistance."

"I expect hostility." Barrett was surprised by a fire simmering low in his belly. He wanted to get into this. He wanted the confrontation. "But come Hell or high water, I'm going to find Danny Robert. And God help them if they've laid a finger on him."

Now they were climbing, following a narrow footpath sketched in the soil. This was probably the route favored by inhabitants of the camp. It was barely visible in places, but someone had taken the trouble to clear away the rocks. At the first turning, Barrett could see them piled off to the side. He wondered how many bags of drugs, stolen TVs and sacks of shoplifted groceries had made their way up via this very route. Approaching the top, the Garbage Messiah's words became more distinct. His voice was thin and reedy, but it held a strange resonance that carried through the night.

"...and we're just getting started! Do you think the Devil's kingdom can be torn down in a day? Or even a *month?* No. It's going to take a lot more effort to pry Satan's machinery from the throat of civilization. But we're the Elect! We're the heroes prepared to make the sacrifices necessary for freedom!"

"Jesus," Kelly muttered. "He's really knitting a flag up there."

"Knitting a flag. Or spinning straw into bullshit. Sometimes they can look an awful lot alike."

"True that."

They topped the rise and stood in the shadows at the edge of the camp. The fire burned high in the metal bowl of a big rig's truck wheel that someone had found and rolled up here. Cardboard boxes, piles of newspaper and strips from wooden pallets also burned fitfully, sending oily smoke streaming into the sky. Barrett was surprised at the size of the group clustered around the firepit. They were hanging on the Garbage Messiah's every word. *There must be twenty or thirty of them,* he thought. All were thin faced, clad in black, with scarred hands and dirty faces, torn backpacks at their feet. Barrett sought for any sign of the ones from the attack behind St. Anne's but the shadows were deep and there were too many unfamiliar faces in the mix. It was as if the Messiah had his own army...

Or congregation...

"It's like prying nails out of a board someone's hammered to a wall!" the Messiah was saying. "You have to pull 'em out one after another. Takes time!"

"C'mon," Barrett whispered. Kelly nodded and they

strode from the shadows together, heading toward the firelight.

"…and we will pry them out—one law, one lie, one authority figure at a time. *Those* are the nails holding the board to our house! And we— Well, well! What do we have here?"

Alerted by his sudden change of pace, the Garbage Messiah's audience turned as one toward Barrett and Kelly as they reached the far edge of the fire light. A silence fell—one so deep that the sound of wood crackling in the flames became as loud as traffic. The Garbage Messiah, clad in jeans and a blue work shirt, stood grinning through his long, scraggly beard, hands on his hips, relishing this unexpected moment of drama in his private kingdom.

"Hey!" he said. "Lookie here! We got not just one, but *two* black coats! How about that?"

"We're here looking for someone," Kelly said, chin raised, her voice pitched to a no-nonsense tone. "Someone who's gone missing."

"Well, ain't that a shame?" The Messiah's voice swelled with insincere concern. "But you know. Things go missing all the time. Pens. Pencils. Socks. Cigarette lighters. It's important to know when and where to let go!"

"Has Danny Robert been here?" Barrett fired the question at the Messiah from directly behind Kelly's shoulder. "We need to know."

"'*We need to know.*'" The Garbage Messiah's tone sharpened as he mocked Barrett's words. "You think I give a shit what you *need*, pedo? How about I rip your cock off and stuff in that lady preacher's mouth before I crucify her?"

"You're one sick fucker," Kelly snapped. Barrett could feel the rage coming off her in waves.

A murmur rose among the assembled faithful. The woman 'black coat' had gone too far. Who was she to question the Messiah? Threatening tones and glances were fired their way. And the Messiah gloried in their antagonism, in the rising tide of hate swelling among his followers.

"Yes...*yes!*" He waved his arms like a man conducting an orchestra. "You, the Elect! You understand! You know what *must be done!*"

A group of about five surged to their feet and began advancing on Kelly. The Garbage Messiah moved to join them.

"I WANT HER HEAD!" he screeched, pointing.

Barrett drew the Glock, raised it skyward, and fired. Immediately, the surge of disciples headed toward them stopped.

"Well!" The Garbage Messiah seemed mildly impressed. "Lookie here! A black coat with a *gun!* Ain't that a break in your holy vows of nonviolence, father?"

"So's murder," Barrett snapped, swinging the gun around and centering the sights on the Messiah's forehead. "But I'll take the L."

The silence that followed was broken by the wail of sirens.

Barrett grinned tightly.

That's Gavin. Headed this way. With backup.

"Before this is over," Barrett vowed to the Garbage Messiah, "I'm going to fucking kill you."

He and Kelly moved back into the shadows and found the path down the hill as Lewis' Crown Vic swept toward the Dump, followed by two other police cars.

The Abyss

"JESUS! LOOK AT THEM SCATTER!" Kelly half-turned to Barrett from the driver's seat, her hand on the wheel as she marveled at the sight beyond the windshield. "Like a flock of damn crows!"

"A murder," Barrett corrected. "A group of crows is called a murder."

"Well then, the Garbage Messiah's meeting was an attempted murder 'cuz they're sure as hell scattering now!"

She was right. In the road ahead and on the slope just off to their right, a wave of black clad figures carrying backpacks or dragging shopping carts was rushing downhill toward town. From up top, the blue and red lights of police cars pulsated into the night.

"Gavin and his fellow horsemen have hit the camp." Barrett paused as she slowed to allow a pair of homeless to sprint past. "A direct frontal assault on the Garbage Messiah's kingdom."

"Well, if there's to be an escalation, it's better that our side start it." Kelly narrowed her eyes, casting a critical gaze over the retreating horde. For a moment, Barrett could see the former infantry officer in her. "That bastard has declared war on this town and its people. And our *churches* in particular. And we're both willing to take a bullet for that." With a tone of admiration directed his way, she added: "Or insert a bullet into the enemy. You did good back there, Barrett. We could have used you in Kandahar."

"I was busy fighting terrorists in Toronto. The terrorists within the Roman Catholic Church. But thanks." Barrett wondered how many of the Garbage Messiah's flock Lewis and his fellow Mounties would manage to round up. If the blizzard of black clad homeless was any indication, not too many.

Seeing a man hurtling down the slope in their direction, Kelly slowed again.

"We had our share of hairy moments in the Red Zone," he said.

"Hookers? Junkies? Mental cases?"

"Yep. And plenty of ordinary, decent, law-abiding folks who just freaked. You know what they say. We're all just one bad day away from becoming a danger to society."

"You're preaching to the choir, Barrett. Any idea how many vets end up in jail for just that reason?"

"Jesus. I don't wanna know…"

Suddenly, a lone figure materialized before the hood of Kelly's Bug. She snapped on the brakes scant seconds before she would have ploughed him down, burying him beneath the steel hood and crushing him to bits under the low chassis. But instead, she stopped such that he and his features were ignited in the weird orange blaze from the headlamps but obscured by the night and fog. His closeness to the source of illumination smeared his features in a mask that was weirdly misshapen and surreal. But there was no doubting who it was.

"Garbage Messiah," Barrett breathed. He wanted to tell her to floor it, to run the rotten song-of-a-bitch down. But that was her call.

She didn't. They remained at a standstill, scant yards from his knees. In the VW's glowing headlamps, the Garbage Messiah raised his right hand skyward in a fist and then brought it down hard onto the hood, denting Kelly's car.

She squared her jaw, joggled the gear shift to neutral, and floored the accelerator.

The Bug's turbocharged 20-valve engine roared like an enraged grizzly bear in heat, bellowing its challenge across the scant yards between it and the Garbage Messiah's knees. Kelly was mad as hell and done fucking around with this son-of-a-bitch. Barrett knew the signs. If they were face-to-face right now, she'd be grasping him by the throat.

Instead, she pumped the accelerator, bellowing at him via the one-score valve engine, roaring automotive defiance, blasting exhaust and gas fumes into his face. She punched the pedal with her foot and the engine roared again. And the Garbage Messiah's Rasputin face widened in a horrific grin.

"That son-of-a-bitch is actually getting off on this." The voice with which Kelly spoke these words was flatly clinical and chilling to Barrett. He knew that somehow within the last thirty seconds the Garbage Messiah had changed, in her sight, from being a human to becoming a target. She was prepared to floor the accelerator. Grind the son-of-a-bitch under her wheels. Barrett understood and, at some level, couldn't blame her. But he still had a priestly duty.

"Kelly. Thou shalt not kill."

"Yeah?" She was breathing heavily. "How about *thou shalt have no other Gods before Me*' and, if so, what does that make this son-of-a-bitch?"

"Okay. Yeah. Sure." Barrett had to admit she had a point. The Garbage Messiah *had* set himself up as some flesh-and-blood icon. He wore the false authority of holy 'writ' about himself like a poisoned garland. He was an unholy idol if ever there was one.

The Garbage Messiah abruptly turned and lumbered off into the shadows alongside the road. He, like so many of his followers, had evaded Lewis' clumsy dragnet and were now headed toward town. For what purpose, the Garbage Messiah alone knew.

Kelly turned to Barrett. "So, what do we do now?"

"Let's head into town. Cruise along the main drag. Give Lewis a hand."

"Give him a *hand?*"

"Well, where do you think law enforcement is right now?"

"Well, up on the... Oh, I see."

She steered the VW into town. The streets were mostly still although now and then, black shadows flitted around doorways and the mouth of alleyways like stygian moths. Barrett knew what was going on. With law enforcement at the mound, it meant a free-for-all in Fulton. As he put this all together, he felt Kelly's intuition, honed on foreign battlefields, narrow into focus like a sniper's eyes behind gun sights. She knew trouble was coming. She was braced for trouble coming. And she was ready to give trouble back.

The sound of gunshots snapped somewhere in the darkness ahead.

"Hit it!" snapped Barrett.

Kelly floored it. And a moment later, they were speeding toward trouble.

———

THEY ROARED PAST THE JUNCTION. The bar's interior was still lit but quiet on this particular night. Two blocks beyond lay the parking lot of the Fulton Arms Motor Hotel. Something about the angle at which one of the cars was parked set off alarm bells in the back of Barrett's mind. He tapped Kelly's arm and pointed. She slowed. The sounds of the gunfire were louder and coming from somewhere close to the motel.

Kelly brought the Bug to a halt in the lee of a brick apartment building at the edge of the motel parking lot. They rolled out and advanced to the perimeter of the lot, hugging the apartment's brick wall. The gunfire had paused and now they could hear voices, one of which was raised in anger. Kelly came to the building's edge and stopped. She took a chance and peered around the corner then turned back to him.

"Two of the Messiah's people. I recognize them from the Dump. They're armed."

"Hunting rifles?" Barrett drew his Glock.

"Yeah. They're posted up behind that car, the one parked parallel to the office entrance."

"Let me take a look."

Kelly shrank back to let Barrett approach and peer around the edge of the building himself. He could see the two armed disciples in their black hoodies crouching behind a sedan, facing the office doorway in which stood the owner, a fat hairy man in a wife-beater t-shirt holding a Remington pump action rifle in his hands.

"Didn't count on me being here, did ya'?" he snarled

at them. "Well, I *live* right behind the office! Tryna' come in for the cash box? Ya' junkie *fucks!*"

"Just throw it out to us!" barked the male disciple, his chipped teeth and filthy blonde beard visible in the light of the motel lot. "Just give us what we want!"

"YOU CAN GO STRAIGHT TO HELL!"

"We both will!" The bearded disciple was racking the slide on his rifle. The hotel owner, seeing this, ducked back inside. A moment later, the snout of his weapon poked out from the shadowed doorway.

"Jesus," Barrett said. "It's the gunfight at the OK Corral in there."

"We need cops. We need backup," she said.

"Here." Barrett handed over his cellphone. "You'll find Gavin Lewis' number in there. That's his private number, his cellphone. Call him and fill him—"

His next words were drowned out by gunfire. Barrett could see lights going on in the windows of the apartment buildings next door. Soon the switchboard would be flooded with calls for police. At least Kelly's would give Lewis good onsite intel, and a sense of what they were walking into. Barrett moved back to the corner of the building, both hands on the Glock's grip, its barrel pointed toward the ground.

The bearded disciple continued firing over the hood toward the office, shattering the front windows, causing a rain of triangular glass shards to smash on the pavement below. As he blasted off another salvo, the woman was working her way around to flank the motel owner's position. Kelly, meanwhile, was on the phone behind him.

"...two assailants. Both armed. They're—yeah. Homeless from the camp at the Dump. Armed with hunting rifles."

"Tell him the hotel owner is armed and returning fire," Barrett urged.

As she relayed this, Barrett considered the situation. It would take a unit time to get here. And meanwhile the female disciple was closing in on the perfect spot from which to snipe dead the motel owner as he returned fire. It was time to take action. Barrett raised the Glock, found the trigger, and blasted the passenger side mirror off the car just in front of her.

The woman started, jumped, and spun. Her eyes found him. A second before she was returning fire and retreating behind a panel van.

"Okay." Kelly snapped shut the phone. "They're on their way. The—"

The wail of sirens broke in the darkness around them. The cavalry was coming. But the duo in the parking lot weren't quite ready to cut and run.

The one with the beard rose and spoke again. "Throw out that cash box now or else we're throwing a Molotov cocktail in there!"

The motel owner did not argue He merely returned fire, blasting away until the bearded man ducked. A few shots came from behind the panel van then fell silent. The scream of the sirens was everywhere now. Any second the police would arrive...

That's when they chose to cut and run. First the woman, then the man rose and sprinted to the far edge of the motel lot and disappeared around the far corner of the building. Barrett straightened and holstered his Glock. Three police cruisers, lights and sirens going, swept into the motel parking lot.

The motel owner stepped out, rifle in his hands, and pointed in the direction the pair had run. But the cop from the nearest cruiser stepped out, held up a gloved hand, and barked:

"Put *down* the *rifle!*"

The motel owner started and laid the weapon on the ground. The young cop moved in and cuffed him. Then he bent and retrieved the weapon, guiding the motel owner to the back seat of the cruiser. Barrett and Kelly watched as he closed the man in then placed his Remington in the trunk.

"So much for stand-your-ground laws in Canada," muttered Kelly.

Barrett had to admit she had a point. He could see Gavin conferring with the other Mountie from Campbell River by the motel office door. Then he felt Kelly's hand on his arm.

"Let's go," she suggested.

"You serious?"

"Sure." She shrugged. "We've done our bit. We reported the shooting. They're on top of this. They don't need us. We don't have to get involved if we don't want to."

It was true. With these cops in from out of town, Lewis wasn't counting on Barrett the way he usually did. Perhaps this was a chance to lay low and avoid the field of fire for a change.

"Yeah, let's go," he murmured finally.

They backed up the shadowy street to her car.

Crimes & Misdemeanors

BARRETT PULLED into the driveway of the rectory, switched off the Hyundai and leaned his head against the steering wheel.

The entire town was going to hell.

His specific area of responsibility – legally and professionally, at any rate – was his church and parishioners. From a personal standpoint, it was his friends Gavin, Walton and now Kelly. Beyond that…?

To hell with this town, he thought, getting out of the car. He formed the thought in his mind, but it sat without conviction. Like it or not, there was a part of him that *was* starting to care about Fulton. Maybe not about the municipality itself, but some of the people who lived here. He cared about the Chief and his tribe. He cared about Miss Dolan and the lady who rang up his boxed wine at the liquor store. And he cared about the activity coordinators at the community center from whom he occasionally rented space. But…

To hell with this town.

Telling himself he didn't care, Barrett let himself into

the kitchen. The house was quiet, the lights half-dimmed. Miss Dolan was hours gone. And for now, the only sound Barrett heard was the faint buzz of the TV in the guestroom. That meant Radcliffe was still up—and not in Barrett's office!

He rushed downstairs. And, lo and behold, it was true! His office was unoccupied!

Switching on the light, he surveyed the room. All the junk and detritus had been cleared away and there was some evidence that vacuuming had occurred. Barrett even detected the tell-tale swipe-trails of Miss Dolan's dusting cloth. Yes, the housekeeper had been thorough about tidying up after Radcliffe's lengthy occupation. There was almost no trace whatsoever of his presence...

Except for the stack.

Barrett sat and examined the tower of print-out paper by the printer. A hundred—possibly two hundred —typewritten pages. This must have been Radcliffe's 'project.' Barrett was hesitant to touch it. The damn thing was Radcliffe's, after all. His first impulse was to collect the thing and march it upstairs, lay it quietly by the doorway to the guestroom for the archbishop to retrieve. But then again...

He *was* curious.

Of course, it wasn't his place to intrude on somebody else's work. But Radcliffe *was* his houseguest. And, what was more, his *responsibility*. It made a proprietary sort of sense, from a caretaker standpoint, to at least *familiarize* himself with the contents. Only in a very general way of course. But just in case Radcliffe suffered some sort of mental breakdown. The doctors might want to know what his preoccupations had been. So, in a sense, it was Barrett's *duty*...

Oh, horseshit!

...to understand what his guest was concerned about. To know his anxieties. Because he *was* elderly. And obviously of enfeebled mind. So Barrett *should*...

Stop it!

He compromised by gathering up the papers and marching upstairs to the kitchen where he laid them on the table before grabbing a fresh mugful of wine. As he took a sip, his eyes caught a passage of text.

...was preparing to invest funds in a financial venture— a small holiday resort. The property near the lake had remained undeveloped for years and was ideally located to take advantage of the yearly influx of tourists to the area. Investors had settled upon the name 'Shady Acres.'

Barrett started, remembering his conversation with Gavin.

"You remember Shady Acres?"

"You mean that little collection of holiday cottages out by the lake?" Barrett nodded. *"The ones Squatch used to break into?"*

"Yep. Those are the ones. Anyway, Gordon and Louise kept bringing them up. Not sure why..."

Gordon and Louise...

Barrett gathered together and straightened up the stack. Then he took a seat at the table and began reading.

———

IT WAS midnight when he finished.

He felt the sudden urge—a *need,* even—to move. He got up from his chair, stepped outside the kitchen door, and lit a cigarette.

He was trembling.

Barrett remembered what Crowe had said about wanting to move Radcliffe in, keep him under wraps and then move him out as quickly as possible. Barrett remembered some reference to 'wrongdoing' during their conversation.

'Wrongdoing' is one hell of a euphemism for what he did!

Barrett finished his cigarette, ground it out underfoot and crept upstairs.

He walked softly down the hallway to the door of the guestroom and peered inside. Beneath a rumpled heap of sheets and blankets, Radcliffe snored peacefully. The TV had been switched off over an hour ago. Barrett knew he would get very little satisfaction from waking him up and questioning him about the contents of the short book he had composed and left in Barrett's office. But its contents were lucid enough, even if the man composing them seemed a bit potty. What was beyond question was that Radcliffe was a bad guy.

"Prince of the church," Barrett muttered angrily.

Part of him wanted to step into the room and hold a pillow over Radcliffe's face until he stopped breathing. But, of course, he wouldn't do that. Murdering a house-guest was hardly Christian behavior. But Radcliffe had to pay for what he had done. Somehow.

Softly, Barrett closed the door, pulled the hasp over the ring and sealed Radcliffe in with the new lock he had purchased. Then he returned downstairs.

Crowe had questions to answer. Barrett would see to it. Crowe's position as the current archbishop absolved him of nothing. He was partially responsible for the disaster that had befallen Gordon and Louise and the other members of the tribe – a disaster that was entirely man-made and completely unnecessary.

He sat down at the table, straightened the stack of papers and began re-reading them in their entirety.

———

"I SEE you've locked the archbishop back up in the guestroom, father." Miss Dolan made her statement the next morning sound like an innocent observation but Barrett wasn't buying it. A year of her hen-pecking had taught him that a tacit accusation lurked behind just about every word she spoke. Miss Dolan gleefully inhabited that saintly space where she never exactly condemned anyone but rather cast her rhetorical nets such that arguing with her threw doubt upon one's rectitude.

"Yes." Barrett smiled sadly as he poured coffee into his mug then bent to the fridge in search of creamer. "Sadly, it became necessary. For his own good, you understand."

"And how is that, father?" she asked, self-righteously adjusting the straps if her apron. "What could Archbishop Radcliffe have done that would necessitate incarcerating him in the guestroom for his own good?"

"Well…" Barrett paused, creamer in hand, and glanced this way and that, as if preparing to share a dangerous confidence. "Miss Dolan. Can I trust you to keep something just between the two of us?"

"Oh, most certainly, father," she said, beaming. As Barrett suspected, the woman was an inveterate gossip. No doubt whatever he said would soon be put in circulation among the parish in general.

"Archbishop Radcliffe was involved in an unprovoked attack on some members of our local First Nations." He held up a hand. "I know he seemed safe when you let him out yesterday. And thank God nothing happened. But Miss Dolan, you must understand. Archbishop Radcliffe is an extremely violent and dangerous man."

Miss Dolan's expression became one of absolute bewilderment. Barrett cheered inwardly.

"It's a terrible thing, truth be told." Barrett smirked as he reflected that what he said was not exactly a lie, merely a creative elaboration on the truth. "I'm about to arrange a meeting with Archbishop Crowe about it. I suspect we'll see him sometime later today or tomorrow. Be sure you leave him locked up. For your own safety."

"Saints preserve us, father..." She crossed herself.

Barrett bit back laughter as he headed down the stairs to his office.

———

HE ANSWERED A FEW E-MAILS, then walked over to the church to perform morning Mass for a handful of die-hard Catholics. Afterwards, he finished off the Communion wine in the vestry and wondered about Danny Robert's whereabouts as he studied the newly repaired window. Then he returned to his home office. The call from Crowe came shortly after lunch.

"Mike? Andrew Crowe here. Brother Steven mentioned you phoned." Crowe's voice was tinny and distant. Barrett could hear the hubbub of what sounded like an airport terminal in the background. "How are things going with Archbishop Radcliffe?"

"Honestly, not well." Barrett swished wine in his mouth as he chose his next words. "Andrew, I think it's time to talk about Archbishop Radcliffe's tenure in office. And about your time here as parish priest."

"What about it, Mike?"

Barrett took a deep breath. And told him.

———

I WONDER *how he'd feel,* Barrett thought as he watched the taxi pull up in front of the house, *if he knew that Kelly Ward and I were drinking and…*

Crowe got out of the cab, pulled a garment bag from the backseat and paid the driver.

And doing other things together.

It didn't matter. Because Crowe would never find out about those things. And whatever guilt Barrett might be feeling about them had become firmly and fully squelched by what he had discovered reading Radcliffe's confession.

"Your excellency. Andrew." Barrett smiled and extended a hand. "Good to see you."

"Mike." Crowe sighed, set down his garment bag, and stretched. "I had to re-arrange my schedule to get here. But it turns out to be a good thing. This trip has been a crusher. I could use a day or two as a break."

"Hmm. I've put on some coffee."

Barrett led Crowe into the kitchen and sat him down at the table. "Miss Dolan has made a plate of fudge brownies. Care for one?"

"Certainly. Thanks." Crowe took off his jacket and began polishing his spectacles. It was the first time, Barrett reflected, he had ever seen Crowe without them. "Will Archbishop Radcliffe be joining us?"

"No." Barrett set down the coffee and brownie before Crowe then took a seat himself. "I wanted to speak to you alone."

"I figured." Crowe replaced his glasses and sat

perfectly still, his coffee and brownie untouched. Waiting.

"I didn't know that the Church had invested in the Shady Acres resort cottages," Barrett began, trying to keep things smooth.

Crowe bit his lips, looked down at his plate, and waited a beat before answering. "We were initial investors, Mike. I was the one who brought it to the archbishop's attention. I had heard about it from Arnold McLellan. Radcliffe was enthusiastic. Took personal charge of the initiative. I introduced him to members of the local business community."

"But they weren't the only investors," Barrett pressed. "And you know it."

Crowe appeared to hesitate for a moment. "There were some investors from the tribe," he said at last.

"Investors from the tribe who got defrauded."

Crowe's face underwent a serial change of expression. Puzzlement became annoyance became resignation. He finally answered, "Yes."

"Radcliffe took their money. Gave them nothing in return. Invested it as his own. And you covered for him."

"I...did."

"Jesus, Andrew!" Barrett threw his head into his hands. "How could you *do* something like that?"

Crowe said nothing.

"So Radcliffe took their money. Invested it as his own. Made a mint, apparently. Shady Acres was quite popular until the late Nineties when it closed. And you...?"

"Took a leave of absence from this parish the moment I learned about it." Crowe pulled off his glasses and pressed his fingertips into his tear ducts. "Mike, I *loved* this parish, this place. Cared deeply for the First

Nations here. I had no desire to leave. But after what happened…" He opened his eyes and spread his hands. "How could I stay?"

"My question is: how could you *return?*"

"I *have* to, Mike. A lot of water has passed under the bridge since then. But the wrong has been done. And it needs to be redressed."

"How?"

"Why do you think I sent him here in the first place?" Crowe smiled. "It's time for him—and me—to be reconciled with the tribe. Time to admit what happened. And make amends."

Escalation

BELLS.

Barrett dreamed he was standing in an empty field. Somewhere in the distance, he could hear church bells ringing...

Bells.

He turned, scanning the distance. The bells were not coming from any particular direction but were picking up speed, now. Ringing more...

Bells.

...frequently, insistently. And at faster intervals. Now it was a mind-splitting cacophony of

Bells.

He jerked awake and glared at the phone on his bedside table. The clock read 2:45 AM. *Really?* He sat up, scrubbed his face with his hands and grappled up the receiver.

"Father Barrett here."

"Mike?" It was Kelly's voice. Instead of her usual confidence, she spoke with a kind of breathless hush. "Mike? Are you there?"

"Kelly." He swung out of bed and put his feet to the floor. "What's going on?"

"Those bastards. Mike, they set my church on fire!"

"I'll be right over."

He hung up and began dressing.

———

HE DROVE like a bat out of hell across town, seeing the pulsing red lights of the fire trucks before even turning down the street where St. Anne's was located. He pulled up across from the church, parking in a position to give maximum clearance for emergency vehicles. The volunteer fire department was already on site, a command vehicle and a ladder truck pulled up on the lawn in front of the modern A-frame façade. Kelly stood in the middle of the road in a t-shirt and jeans, arms folded, shoulders hunched as she watched the firemen dragging a hose across the sidewalk toward the church.

"Hey." Barrett put a hand on her arm. "You okay?"

"Yeah." She gripped his hand in her own. "Thank God for smoke alarms. I was dead to the world, Mike. Out cold in dreamland when all of a sudden the damn thing starts shrieking. I woke up and a cloud of smoke came wafting downstairs. Jesus, I could have…"

"Shh. It's okay." Barrett pulled her to him in a tight hug. The firemen positioned the hose and switched on the nozzle, directing a stream of water toward the fitfully burning wooden hutch where St. Anne's garbage and recycling cans were stored. It looked as if the arsonists had started the fire there. Streaks from the flames had clawed the side of the building, leaving black scars which stopped just short of the roof. Had that caught fire,

Barrett knew, it would have been game over for the whole church.

"When I got outside, I saw them." Her words frosted over with rage. "About six of the little black-clad fuckers, taking off across the lawn. One held a gas can."

The incident commander approached, splashing through streams of water running out onto the street, his fire jacket unbuttoned and his helmet pushed back on his head.

"Garbage fire," he assured them. "They doused your trash and recycling cans with gasoline, lit them up, and *poof!* If your call had come in five minutes later, your church would be ashes. As it stands, we're doing flash suppression right now. I'd like to do a walk-through of the place if you don't mind. Just to be sure."

"Help yourself," said Kelly, handing over the keys. "And thanks."

"You're welcome, reverend." The fireman considered his next words carefully. "Once we're done here, you should call Sergeant Lewis at the RCMP detachment. My investigation isn't complete yet but there's no doubt at all this was an act of arson."

"Kelly witnessed the suspects fleeing during the fire," said Barrett. "They've been harassing both of us and our churches. We may know a few by sight."

"Okay. Good. We'll finish up here, let you get back inside to air the place out. I'll call Gavin myself in the morning."

"Thank you," said Kelly.

As they stood watching the incident commander enter the church, Barrett sensed her tensing up beside him. She was fighting back tears.

———

HE PACED BACK and forth in the church vestibule, waiting for Kelly to finish her walkthrough.

We've got to do something about the Garbage Messiah, Barrett thought. *And his army of homeless zombies. We've got to stop the bastard!*

He had seen a light on in the RCMP detachment as he sped by. Lewis was up, doing one of his periodic overnight shifts. Barrett decided to give him a call. He was fishing out his cellphone when Kelly rejoined him.

"We're safe," she said. "The fire chief says there are no hotspots outside and the only thing to be concerned about inside is smoke damage. Our insurance should cover it."

"That's great. More to the point—" He hit Gavin's number on the speed dial. "You're okay. Thank Christ."

"Thank Christ, indeed."

He lifted the phone to his ear. Gavin's phone rang once, twice... It managed five rings before sliding to voicemail. Barrett waited for the beep, then drew in his breath to leave a message when he heard it again.

Gunfire!

Kelly's head snapped around. "Small arms!" she snapped. "Downtown!"

"Jesus!" Barrett cut off the call, jammed his cell into a pocket and grasped Kelly's hand. They ran outdoors. Sure enough, rifles were being fired off somewhere close by.

"Come on!"

They got into Barrett's Hyundai and sped toward main street. The lights from the police office threw a rectangle of brightness onto the sidewalk. Barrett drew level and slowed down.

Shattered glass. A kicked-open door. And figures in black flitting in and out of the building.

"Looks like the Garbage Messiah's war against authority has entered a new stage," Kelly said. "What's the play now, Mike?"

———

BARRETT TURNED up the next street and parked close to the intersection. He and Kelly slipped out and made their way toward the police detachment, keeping to the shadows. It occurred to him that the cultural practice of forcing priests to wear black was coming in particularly handy at this moment.

They kept to the sidewalk across the street. He and Kelly crouched low as they moved, taking cover behind parked cars, mailboxes, and sidewalk planters. They crept up to a van that was parked directly opposite Lewis' office. Once behind it, they straightened up, moved to the passenger window, and peered through the cabin toward the open door of the detachment office.

The black clad figures were no longer running in and out, and their number had settled to five. A sixth and final figure was visible—a bearded man clad in a blue work shirt and jeans.

"That's him," said Barrett. "The Garbage Messiah himself."

"Big as life and twice as ugly," muttered Kelly. "I'm guessing he's making his big move?"

"Oh, God," Barrett whispered. "Look! To the right…"

She did and gasped.

Lewis was in there. Obviously at work when the Messiah's minions attacked, he was wearing his duty blouse and pants with the yellow stripe but his gun belt had been removed and he had been forced into a chair, his hands cuffed to the armrests. The Garbage Messiah loomed over him, haranguing Lewis at close range.

"They've taken him hostage," Kelly growled.

"Campbell River RCMP is the nearest detachment. That means backup is two hours away." Frustration bubbled in Barrett's voice.

"What the hell do you think they're going to do with him?"

"They're going to kill him," Barrett said. The cold certainty of it chilled him. The Messiah and his followers had no reason to let Lewis live. No doubt they would taunt and torture him for a period of time before finally offing him.

"We can't let this happen, Mike."

"You're right." Barrett grabbed her arm. "Come on."

———

THEY TOOK a back road out of town into the forest. Ten minutes' travel brought them to a long dirt driveway that led into the trees. They followed it until a split-level cabin appeared in the headlights. Barrett pulled up in front.

"Where are we?" she asked.

"This is Gavin's place." Barrett got out and approached the front door, Kelly at his heels. "Haven't visited in a while, but I seem to remember…"

He climbed the three steps to the porch and looked around. The overhead light was on, the details plain to see. There was Gavin's weathered old wooden rocking chair with the horse blanket over the back, his coffee cup where he'd left it that morning, in its accustomed place on the short stump that functioned as an outdoor table. There was a row of empty clay flowerpots on the railing. Barrett lifted one and withdrew the key beneath it.

"Aw!" Kelly feigned disappointment. "I was hoping to get to see you kick in a door!"

"My door-kicking days are long behind me." Barrett wrestled the key into the lock and opened the place. "Come on."

The interior of Lewis' place resembled a men's club from the Twenties. Overstuffed armchairs, antimacassar tables, and even a spittoon furnished the living room. A drinks trolley nestled by the dining room door. Barrett switched on a lamp with a stained-glass shade.

"There," he said. "Just what the doctor ordered."

A mahogany gun cabinet was on the wall near the fireplace. The thing was ancient – a veritable antique— and probably worth a mint. But its price paled next to the value of its contents. Kelly peered through the glass windows at the hardware within.

"Good God," she whispered.

Gavin, a hunting and outdoors enthusiast, was something of a collector. Ten rifles occupied the cabinet, one for each space on the rack. They represented a range of firearms and were ordered from oldest to most modern. Barrett pulled open the doors.

"Take your pick, Kelly." He smirked. "But I recommend leaving the breech loading musket for another day."

"Man! Is that an M-1?" She pointed in disbelief. "My God, it is! An old, World War II gas-operated model! I'll be damned!"

"He's got some handguns, too." Barrett surveyed the selection. "Now *this*." He reached in and grasped a rifle. "This is a goddam weapon!"

He wrapped his hand around the wooden stock of

the FN FAL, feeling the weight and heft of the thing. Designed in 1953 and chambered for 7.62 rounds, the FN battle rifle was standard issue for NATO troops for years. Dubbed "the right arm of the free world," the FN could unleash 700 rounds per minute from its 30-round detachable box magazine. Barrett drew it out, checked the action, and swept up three box mags from the shelf below the rack.

"I'll take this," Kelly said, taking up a C8. Essentially a miniature M-16, the C8 was standard issue for Canadian military and law enforcement. Barrett knew Gavin carried one in his car. That he had one at home was a surprise. But the fact that he had a few full thirty-round magazines lying around was an even bigger one. Gas operated, with an effective range of 500 meters, the C8 could fire its 5.56 NATO rounds at a velocity of 3,100 feet-per-second.

"Chop down trees with this baby," she said, admiring the gleaming rifle in her hands. "And he's got a sling for it, too. Hot damn!" she said, shouldering her way into the nylon accessory and clipping the rifle to it.

"Here." He picked up and handed over one of two Browning 9mm handguns on the shelf before taking the second for himself and stuffing it into the waistband of his pants. Kelly suddenly laughed.

"That's something you don't see very often," she said.

He turned in the direction she pointed. In the full-length mirror by the hall door, he caught sight of the two of them. Both dressed in their clerical uniforms, they stood holding their assault rifles like a pair of latter-day Christian ninjas.

"This is us," Barrett said with a smirk.

"Fuckin' A." Kelly racked the slide of her C8. "C'mon, Mike. Let's go *get some*."

War

THEY AGREED HITTING the front and back doors simultaneously would be their best bet. Barrett let Kelly take the lead on tactics. "Front or back?" he asked.

"You take the front," she said. "You they'll be expecting. I'll let my appearance come as a surprise."

"They'll probably have the back door covered."

Kelly reached down to her ankle, pulled up her pantleg and produced a long, black titanium dagger from an ankle sheath.

That wasn't something she put on at Gavin's, he thought. *Does she carry that on the regular?*

"I've totally got it under control," she assured him quietly.

———

THEY DID one more round of reconnaissance, keeping to the shadows across the street until reaching the panel van. A glance through the cabin windows told them what they needed to know.

The force had split. Gavin remained in the front room, cuffed to his office chair. The Garbage Messiah was still there haranguing him. Two disciples as well. The other two smoked outside the front door.

"The fifth will be covering the back," she whispered. "Give me five minutes to get into position. I'll move when you move." She extended a fist. "Good hunting."

Barrett bumped it and she was off, moving soundlessly through the shadows toward the back door.

———

FRAGMENTS of the Garbage Messiah's rap filtered out to him as he waited. It was the same jive he'd been spinning up at the campfire, delivered in a fast-talking, huckster tone. He was knitting his flag again.

"...just the beginning, man! We start here. And it *spreads*. Once people see what can be done... Man, how long do you think it will take the Indians to start storming little outposts like yours? They got a real hate on for you red-coats!"

Lewis, eyes on the floor, mouth firm, said nothing. He had been trained in RCMP Depot to maintain composure even under the most withering fusillade of insults and provocations. Barrett knew he had been in more than a few tight spots before – several life-threatening. But he couldn't imagine it was easy for him to bear this.

"We're free men on the land, jack!" The Garbage Messiah's voice rose loud enough to echo down the street. "You can't take that from us! You've tried, but you can't! So now you and all the other people who live inside will pay. The. Price."

Barrett gripped and regripped the handle of his FN.

Its safety was off, its selector switch set to semi-auto. And the Messiah's two minions had turned to face inward toward the office.

Five minutes had passed.

It was now or never.

Barrett swept out from behind the panel van, moving on the balls of his feet, the FN up and pointed at a spot between the shoulder blades of the nearest disciple. He made it to within ten feet and stopped. Their attention remained on the Messiah. They had no idea he was behind them.

Three things happened simultaneously.

Barrett squeezed off and put down the nearest disciple.

The Garbage Messiah looked out the window and saw him.

And gunfire erupted from the back door.

Barrett swung the snout of the FN toward the second man. He was turning, too, hands fumbling for the hunting rifle he had let go and allowed to dangle by its strap upside-down. He brought it up incorrectly, its trigger pointed up, its barrel parallel with the ground. And yet he still somehow managed to fire it. The bullet went wide and was enough to cause Barrett to flinch away.

From inside, more gunfire. The Garbage Messiah had turned toward the back door…

The disciple, meanwhile, was trying to turn his rifle right-way up. Barrett put a bullet through his skull and made for the open doorway.

The disciple in the room with the Messiah was on his feet and charging toward the back door. Barrett reached the jamb in time to put a bullet through his skull. Barrett thought he heard Kelly's voice raised, then another gunshot. But his focus was on the Messiah now.

He spun inward to see the Garbage Messiah hauling Gavin across the room on his office chair. Barrett threw the FN to his shoulder and sighted on the Messiah's head.

"Hold it, you son-of-a-bitch!"

The Garbage Messiah drew a straight razor from his pocket, opened it, and held the blade to Gavin's throat. The Messiah opened his mouth to speak when suddenly one of his disciples burst in through the back door. Barrett clocked his entrance an instant before he stumbled and fell face-down into the main room, Kelly on his back, her dagger inserted into his ribs from behind. The disciple died, squirming on the floor and gurgling blood.

She looked up. "Three down," she said calmly.

"And I got two." Barrett returned his attention to the Garbage Messiah. "Which leaves us with you, sweetheart."

"Sweetheart, eh?" The Messiah cocked his head. "You priests really love that sexy talk, donchya'? Must be all part of that blue balls celibacy thing. Now—ah, *ah* there, sweetheart!" He pushed the razor's edge right up under Gavin's chin and addressed Kelly. "You just lay that little pig sticker of yours down right there by Jerry. Poor disciple Jerry. He was a good and faithful servant."

Kelly, breathing slowly, placed her titanium dagger exactly where the Garbage Messiah bid her, her movements calm, deliberate and slow. When she was done, she kept her hands raised.

"Now back off, little lady. And you, man." The Messiah grinned. "Put down your weapon."

"Mike!"

Kelly's voice was strangled with fear. Then Barrett

saw it, the thin trickle of blood dripping from the razor's edge. The Garbage Messiah had the blade positioned such that with one swipe, he would open Gavin's throat and end it all right there for the Mountie.

Barrett had a choice to make. He could comply. Or he could take the shot. If he chose to do so and the bullet connected, there was a good chance that the blade would sink deep into or fly right through the skin of Lewis' neck as the Messiah's hand spasmed in death. And Barrett knew he didn't have much time on hand to make that call. So he weighed it all out in his mind, deciding there were too many check-marks in the 'con' column. He sighed.

"Okay, okay," he said quietly. "I'm putting the rifle down."

"Okay, then!" The Messiah's school marm tone couldn't hide the flush of relief he felt at having gotten away with his gambit.

Barrett lowered the FN, dropped his left hand from the front stock, letting the rifle dangle from his right before dropping and kicking it away into a corner of the room.

"You win," he told the Garbage Messiah calmly. He raised his hands. "You're in control now. Tell us what to do."

"Well, you're well on your way to giving me everything I want, black coat," said the Messiah. "And lookie here. I've got not just one but *two* of the authority figures in town under my thumb." He lifted the razor from Gavin's throat to gesture with it. "If I have both the law and the church in my hands, what does that make me?"

"A criminal psychopath?" answered Barrett.

"Wrong, spooky!" The Messiah glared. "Makes me a king!" He laughed harshly. "A goddam *king!* When you are the head of the church and the head of state all at once…"

"The Pope is the head of our church."

"Yeah well, he ain't *here,* is he?" the Messiah hissed and swept the blade back into place below Gavin's chin. "Come to think of it, neither are any more Mounties! Why do you think I chose this place, hoss? I figured I should start small. Conquer an isolated place I could use as a base of operations."

"For what?" Barrett asked.

"From which to run my worldwide revolution!"

"You're ambitious. I'll give you that." Barrett looked over the Messiah's shoulder and out the window beyond. There lay the silent sidewalks of Fulton, likely to remain unused for another few hours yet. Just a single curious passerby could change the game entirely. But it simply wasn't going to happen. Barrett settled for telling the Messiah, "You're out of your frigging mind, pal."

"Says the apostle of everyone's favorite invisible playmate!" The Garbage Messiah's eyes twinkled with mirth. "What do you peddle, *priest?* Just more lies. False comfort. The status quo. Have you done anything? Anything at *all*…"

The hand holding the razor reached skyward, gesturing for emphasis.

"…to live up to the revolutionary promise of your founder?"

And Kelly's Browning roared.

———

BARRETT TWITCHED at the sound of the shot. But for the weight at the small of his back, he might have forgotten passing out the sidearms from Gavin's gun cabinet. Kelly had picked her moment and chosen well. The razor was away from Gavin's neck. The Garbage Messiah had offered maximum exposure of his own center mass. Everything had lined up for the perfect shot. But that's not how it went down.

Her bullet missed its target by bare inches, grazing the Garbage Messiah's ribs on the way past. He cried out and twitched back but remained on his feet. The bullet sped past him and shattered the window that looked out onto the sidewalk.

The Messiah took that opportunity to fling the straight razor at Kelly. Her reaction was instinctive, flinching back from the straight edge whirling its way through the air toward her. The muzzle of her Browning was no longer on him but pointing at the ceiling.

And that's when the Garbage Messiah made his move, grasping the edge of the shattered window and vaulting through, landing on the sidewalk outside. Then Barrett could hear his footsteps pounding up the street into the distance.

"There's a handcuff key in my desk!" Gavin cried. "Top drawer."

Barrett stepped over and yanked it open. The cuff key was in the stationery tray, atop the paperclips. He pulled it out and handed it over to Kelly, then bent to take up the FN.

"You go after him!" Lewis said as she bent to unfasten a cuff. "We'll be right behind you!"

Barrett sprinted through the doorway and up the sidewalk after the Messiah.

Darkness. Silence. The swishing panorama of the streets as he hurtled past, flashing a look up and down each intersection to see where the man might have fled. To be sure, the Messiah was fast, being a past master at such urban track races. But he had no idea that Barrett was a seasoned hunter.

There!

Scuffed gravel at the foot of an alleyway, the suggestion of a shoe sliding through grit and sand. Someone had made a fast turn around this corner. Barrett flattened himself against the wall and listened...

Tick, tick, tick...

Distant footsteps. The Messiah had turned here and was making for...

Where?

Barrett rounded the corner and oriented himself. This alley ran straight the way through the back end of town, ending in the industrial area around Crowley Street. Well and good. That meant...

He's heading home.

The Garbage Messiah was making for the Dump. The move made a certain kind of tactical sense. The Messiah knew his time in Fulton was over, so the moment had come to gather up either his ditty bag or weapon and either split or mount an armed resistance. Barrett couldn't be sure which seemed more likely.

But one thing was clear. The Garbage Messiah would not be allowed to succeed at either.

Barrett paused to check his rifle. Then he knelt and put it aside before going over the Browning. Satisfied both were in good working order, he stowed the pistol, took up the FN and went after his quarry.

Crucifixion

HE WAS outside the nimbus of town lights, now. His shadow—head, torso, and a pair of arms cradling the FN—slipped up the road ahead of him, lengthening until it was a surreal parody of the human form before vanishing entirely. There were no streetlights out this far – just darkness, unbroken by variances of light and shadow. The Messiah had chosen his roosting grounds well: out of sight, out of mind, safe beyond the reach of law and order.

Beyond the reach of Man's law, he corrected himself.

Barrett was preparing to deliver a different kind of justice.

Flickers of light pulsated from the top of the hill where the Messiah and his minions made camp. That they should have a fire burning at this hour, especially after what had transpired, seemed foolhardy. Surely, they knew it was just a matter of time before Lewis charged in bearing the full weight of the Crown's wrath. So why the light?

He's probably stoked up a dying fire and is just using the light to pack up, Barrett thought. *Or arm up.*

Either way, it made no difference. Barrett intended to end him.

His phone buzzed. A text from Kelly.

Campbell River sending a tactical response team by chopper. They're 20 minutes out.

Barrett nodded. An Emergency Response Team, loaded with automatic weapons and SWAT gear, would tilt the balance decisively in their favor. He was still thinking this when her follow-up text arrived.

You better not get yourself killed, mister.

He smiled and started up the hill toward the fire.

————

THE NARROW, rutted path was unguarded. Barrett picked his way carefully along the trail, keeping an ear open for voices. He knew Lewis would be along soon, and that the canny old Mountie wouldn't come with lights and sirens. He'd come quietly, the way he went after elk. Because Barrett knew he wanted the Garbage Messiah as badly as he did.

He reached the top of the hill. The stillness there was unnerving, a total contrast from Barrett's last visit. The tents and lean-to shelters appeared empty. No groups of black-clad disciples flitted about. There was only a single figure visible the Garbage Messiah himself, kneeling beside the fire pit and poking at the burning lumber with a stick. A backpack lay open beside him, a few items spilling out onto the ground. It looked like he was packing up and getting set to cut trail.

Not going to happen.

Barrett raised the rifle, aimed at the Messiah, and advanced into the firelight.

"Freeze," he said.

The man abruptly froze, like a stop-action pause in a motion picture. Barrett thumbed the FN's safety to OFF. The Messiah smirked when he heard the *click*.

"Thou shalt not kill, Father Barrett," he taunted softly. "Says that right in the Bible."

"It also says '*an eye for an eye and a tooth for a tooth.*'" Barrett steadied his breathing, flexing his fingers around the FN's grip. "Of course, they had more primitive weapons back in Moses' time. That was likely all the damage they could cause."

"That hog-leg you got there is apt to do a lot more than that," said the Garbage Messiah. "You got the stones to kill a man, father? It ain't as easy as it looks on TV."

"What makes you think you'd be my first?"

"Wow! A killer priest, hey?" The Messiah, still kneeling, half-turned, his hands on his thighs. "Like something out of the Crusades!"

"Just think of me as an instrument of God's mercy."

"Oh? You gonna have mercy on me, Father Barrett? How is shooting me merciful?"

"It's merciful to the people of this town," Barrett replied. "You're the one behind it all. The thefts, the assaults. Stabbing that janitor at the community center, that young girl at the church. She was one of your *own*, you sick fuck! Not to mention shooting Walton. Setting St. Anne's on fire. Taking Lewis hostage. Your maniacal plans to 'overthrow authority.' How many bodies need to pile up before you're satisfied?"

"How many bodies have you priests and Mounties piled up in *your* history?"

"So, the mistakes of the past justify your violent rampage?"

"Given those mistakes, what makes your law any better than mine?"

The gunshot sounded somewhere off to the right. Barrett dropped and rolled, bringing the muzzle of the FN to bear on the armed disciple emerging from the tent at the hilltop's edge. He was fighting to re-center his sights on Barrett when Barrett squeezed off. The FN bellowed and punched a round through the man holding the rifle. He slumped.

Garbage Messiah grabbed a flaming stick of wood from the firepit and pitched it at Barrett. As the priest held up an arm to ward it off, the Messiah took advantage of the distraction to sprint to the edge of the hill and disappear over the edge into darkness.

Barrett rose and went after him.

———

BEYOND THE HILLTOP'S EDGE, the plateau crumbled to a scree of stone that descended into shadow. Barrett could hear the crunch of the Garbage Messiah's steps as he fled into the dark. Shifting the FN to his left hand, he lowered himself over the edge onto the stone slope, doing his best to make no sound. A few experimental steps served as a good start but it was impossible to completely muffle his footfalls among the stones. Fortunately, the Messiah was making plenty of racket down below.

There was no footpath through the scree, just a thick coating of stone and shattered rock. Barrett lowered himself cautiously, his grip loosening on the FN such that he nearly lost the rifle at one point. He paused to sling it around his shoulders before continuing. He minimized his own racket by clambering down in a generally diagonal direction, tacking toward level ground. He stepped from the scree and found himself among the piles of discarded items that gave the Dump its name.

How long have people been abandoning stuff here? he wondered. The ground underfoot was a shifting tapestry: bare ground alternating with stretches of empty beer cans and food tins, the broken and discarded box frame of a mattress, piles of furniture and, up ahead, the silhouette of a wrecked automobile – layers of junk archaeology detailing the history and failures of Fulton. Barrett paused and listened.

Silence.

He carefully unslung the FN, checking it by feel. The selector switch was still set to fire, so he moved it to safe against the possibility of a stumble amongst all this junk. The Garbage Messiah was out here somewhere, most likely lying in wait and preparing to spring an ambush. Barrett moved to the edge of an abandoned automobile and peered around. No sign of anyone. He stepped forward—

The blow to the back of his shoulders fell as a massive weight, stunning him. He lost his grip on the rifle and skidded, dropping to his knees. He covered up against the next blow and managed to avoid having his skull ventilated. But whatever was hitting him broke his left wrist with a tart *snap!* Barrett hit the ground and rolled face-up.

The Messiah stood holding a tire iron. He grinned down at Barrett as he loomed against the night sky.

In the distance, they could hear the approaching wail of Lewis' police siren.

And, blessedly, the thrum of an approaching helicopter.

"You're finished," Barrett gasped. "You hear that? It's a tactical response team inbound from Campbell River. Your reign of terror in Fulton is *done*. Party's over, asshole."

"Ha ha ha, you're a funny priest." The Garbage Messiah brandished the tire iron. "They won't catch me. By the time that whirlybird lands, I'll be long gone. But in the time I have left, I'm gonna rid the world of another goddam black coat. I'm gonna bash your head in, man, and dance on the bone fragments until your brain is mush. Leave you as a *warning!*"

"Warning for *what?*"

"Not to mess with the Messiah!" He held the iron aloft. "My garbage! My kingdom! We live in the scraps and shadow of your civilization! We are your *children*, padre. You got that? And every now and then, sooner or later, the children rise up to displace their parents. The world you and your ancestors built will *burn*. And we'll dance in the embers!"

"You're a psychopath."

"And you're a dead man."

"You plan to use that?" Barrett pointed. "When you have a perfectly good automatic weapon lying right there?"

"Say! How about that?" The Messiah dropped the iron rod and picked up the FN. "Nice gun, padre. Is it yours?" He laughed. "Don't matter. It's *mine*, now."

"Well, go ahead and do it, you asshole." Barrett sat upright. "Here. I'll make it easy for you."

The Garbage Messiah threw the FN to his shoulder, sighted, and pulled the trigger.

Click!

Barrett smiled. "Safety's on. Let's see if you can find it before I kill you."

The Garbage Messiah began frantically running his fingers up and down the weapon, searching over the array of toggles and switches. Cradling his broken left wrist on his lap, Barrett reached into his waistband with his right, produced the Browning, and fired a round directly into the Garbage Messiah's left knee. The man plunged to the ground, howling, the FN slipping from his hands to clatter among the trash.

Barrett pushed himself up and limped over to stand above him. For a long moment, the priest remained still, steadying himself. Then he fired, putting a bullet in the Garbage Messiah's right knee.

"You know, Jesus was no doormat," Barrett said grimly. "Oh, sure. He talked all that stuff about forgiveness and turning the other cheek. But when it came to the Pharisees? And the money-changers in the Temple? And demons? He showed. No. Mercy."

Blam! He fired again, shredding the Garbage Messiah's left ankle.

"You harmed my town, my flock, my…*friends,* you Godless, demonic son-of-a-bitch!" Barrett was trembling now, the rage coursing through him so powerfully that he barely felt the pain in his left wrist. He fired again and turned the Garbage Messiah's right ankle into a mass of smoldering bone and flesh.

"I made a promise that I'd kill you before this is all over. It's a promise I intend to keep. But I want you to know as you lie here, writhing in agony during the last minutes of your life that you failed!"

Blam! Barrett shot the man's left wrist.

"*You hear me, you son-of-a-bitch? You failed!*"

Blam! Right wrist.

The Garbage Messiah's face was ivory white with shock. Barrett moved in close and pushed the barrel of the Browning up under his chin.

"Finish me!" begged the Garbage Messiah. "Put a bullet through my brain! Please, father! Please!"

Barrett smiled and stood.

"No," he said quietly.

Then he turned and began picking his way back up through the scree toward the blast and lights of the descending helicopter.

Reconciliation

TWO DAYS LATER, Barrett stood waiting in the driveway for Crowe to conduct Archbishop Radcliffe down from the guest room to the car. His left wrist, swaddled in a bandaged splint, still ached despite the buzz from the painkillers the doctors had proscribed. Judging by the cigarette butts at Barrett's feet, he had been out here for around fifteen minutes. When it came to telling time, cigarette butts never lied. With a sigh, he lit up a fresh one, pulled out his phone and, balancing it awkwardly in his bandaged hand, he sent a text to Kelly.

> Hey there. Taking Radcliffe to the reconciliation meeting now. The last loose end. How are you?

He hit SEND and waited. She replied swiftly.

> Good. Glad it's over. I'm exhausted.

He smiled.

Me, too. Dinner later? My place?

She replied:

Sounds good.

Barrett was still smiling when the kitchen door opened and Crowe appeared, escorting a cleaned-up and freshly-dressed Radcliffe who clung to his arm as they came downstairs to the car. Miss Dolan followed in their wake, clucking and fluttering.

"Now Archbishop Radcliffe, you be sure to come back and visit us again soon," she was saying. "Having you here was such a great pleasure for me and Father Barrett. Truly. You have no idea."

That's right, Miss Dolan, Barrett thought. *He has no idea about that—*

"Ha!"

Or anything else, for that matter…

"Thank you, Miss Dolan." Crowe smiled. "As ever, your excellent service is deeply appreciated by Mother Church."

"Oh, *Archbishop!* Thank *you!*"

Crowe and Barrett bundled Radcliffe into the backseat. As they pulled out of the driveway, Crowe asked: "Still no sign of Danny?"

"No, no sign," Barrett said. "Reverend Ward thought she might have spotted him the other day, but it was just a suspicion."

Crowe sighed. "So that's another thing we'll have to apologize for. Losing a member of their tribe. As if we didn't already have enough to repent for."

Barrett followed the roads to the edge of the reserve and past the signage toward the tribal offices. The large, modern building was one of the newest in town, a two-story cedar office and conference center with glass doors and gleaming stainless-steel fixtures. Barrett's was the only car in the parking lot. As he and the two archbishops approached the lobby, the door opened and the Chief stood there, a warm smile of welcome on his face.

"Father Barrett, it's good to see you," he said. "Thank you for arranging this. And thank you, Archbishop Crowe, for agreeing to come."

"My pleasure, Chief," replied Crowe. "You'll be glad to know that Archbishop Radcliffe is eager to hear what you and Louise Joe have to say. Aren't you, your excellency?"

But Radcliffe was examining the Chief like he'd just seen a ghost. Instead of the usual harsh laugh, he just stood silently, mouth slightly agape. *Is he frightened?* Barrett wondered. Perhaps, but with Radcliffe, who could tell? In the end, the retired archbishop managed to shut his mouth and offer a muttered hello.

"Come on inside," the Chief urged them. "I thought we would talk for a bit before the meeting starts."

He conducted them through a wide lobby with polished stone floors past the reception desk to an office that Barrett assumed must belong to the Chief. It was a large room with an executive style desk, the shelves and wall spaces decorated with Native art and artifacts. It also contained a small, round conference table at which sat another Native man in jeans, jacket and tie. He rose ponderously, a wide-shouldered figure with a weathered face and watchful eyes.

"Father, your excellencies… This is Calvin Leonard, our tribal justice coordinator. He's retired RCMP. He oversees our restorative justice process for the tribe."

Calvin Leonard offered a nod and the ghost of a

smile. Barrett recognized a fellow retired cop when he saw one. Putting an ex-Mountie in charge of the tribal justice office was a smart move on the Chief's part. He imagined Calvin Leonard probably ran excellent interference between the Crown prosecutor's office and the tribe. Leonard took over the meeting as they convened around the small conference table.

"The Chief has briefed me on everything," he said, opening a file before him. "It is my understanding that the retired archbishop, Mr. Radcliffe, wishes to make reconciliation with Louise Joe and the tribe for actions taken many decades ago."

"That is correct, sir," said Crowe. "But it's not just the archbishop that wishes reconciliation. I do, as well. And the Church does."

Leonard listened to this quietly, nodded, and pressed on.

"In a moment, we're going to sit down with Louise Joe and her kin. I'll open the meeting and explain the procedure. But just so we're clear—" He paused. "The issue in question has to do with the misappropriation of funds from the Joe family by Archbishop Radcliffe during his tenure in office. And it's my understanding that the Archbishop has agreed to take responsibility for his wrongdoing. Is that correct?"

"Correct," answered Crowe.

Calvin Leonard paused. "Is the archbishop not capable of speaking for himself?" he asked.

"He's, ah, suffering early onset dementia," said Crowe. "His cognitive abilities are impaired and he can only communicate on a very limited basis. But we've spoken and he's aware of what's going on here. And why it's important to come today. He wants to be here."

"Very well." Leonard turned to the Chief. "I think we're ready to start."

"Alright." The Chief stood. "Let's go into the meeting room."

He conducted them across the lobby to a narrow doorway framed in cedar. The bas reliefs carved into the wood panels on either side of door portrayed traditional Native figures guiding a Dragon boat toward a rocky shoreline. Barrett was absorbed in studying these when Crowe's voice interrupted his reverie.

"Danny!"

Barrett blinked. The door had opened and was being held by Danny Robert. He stood there wearing his typical shy smile. He stood aside to admit the group.

"Where have you been?" Barrett asked. He noted a circle of chairs in the center of the room. Louise and Connie Joe occupied two. Calvin Leonard went over to speak to them as Danny answered.

"Father Barrett, I'm very sorry," he said quietly. "When I heard Archbishop Radcliffe was coming, I went out into the bush and stayed at Grandpa Gordon's old hunting shack by the lake. I had to figure out what to do."

"Is it because…?" Barrett looked over to where Crowe was getting Radcliffe settled in a chair. "Is it because of what happened between him and your family?"

"Yes." Danny's voice was incredibly soft. "When you told me he was coming to stay with you in the rectory, I started having terrible thoughts. Violent thoughts, father. An anger possessed me…"

"You should have told me." Barrett grasped his arm. "Danny, we all care about you! We'd have understood and tried to help."

"No, father. I don't think you would." Danny looked at Barrett's hand until he removed it. "You know my family was very religious? They loved the church, father. Leaving it was very hard on all of them, regardless of the circumstances."

"I see."

"Sometimes, you know, people can ruin a thing for you." Danny's mouth firmed with unusually intense irritation. "Perhaps it's a job or an activity or just a group of people you want to hang around with. But sometimes a person will ruin it so you'll go away because they don't want you around. But it's very different when the thing they ruin for you is your faith community, your relationship with God. Father, that's unforgivable."

Barrett swallowed. Maybe Danny was right. Perhaps he couldn't understand.

"Okay," said Calvin Leonard. "Let's get started."

Barrett and Danny joined the group in the circle of chairs. Barrett noted the exact number of chairs corresponded to the exact number of people present. The only two empty ones left were either next to Radcliffe or Louise Joe. Barrett sighed and settled himself beside the elderly archbishop.

"All set, Archbishop Radcliffe?" he muttered.

"Ha." Radcliffe uttered his favorite exclamation *sotto voce*. It was a good sign that he was at least dimly aware of the circumstances.

"We're gathered today," Calvin Leonard began, "in a circle of reconciliation. Harm has been done. That the circle may be restored to its wholeness, we've gathered to let those who have been harmed speak with those who have caused the harm. We ask that you respect the time of others when it is their turn to speak. We will begin with a prayer."

Everyone stood. The Chief took off his baseball cap and began to speak softly and rapidly in the language of the tribe. Barrett, who didn't understand a word, was moved by the undeniable sincerity of the Chief's tone and facial expressions. He was reaching deep inside himself on behalf of his people. This mattered to him. When he was done, he replaced his cap and they all sat. Calvin Leonard turned to Louise Joe.

"Louise, would you tell us your story?"

The old woman was glaring across the circle at Radcliffe and Crowe. When she spoke, the glare remained fixed and she stayed absolutely still. Only her mouth moved.

"My Gordon was a hard worker," she said. "Hardest working man I ever met. They say Indians are lazy and I suppose some are, but not him. They made fun of him on the road crew. Call him 'Geronimo.' Teased him about drinking even though he never touched a drop of alcohol. Nobody in our family ever did. He was a man who took his role as a father and provider very seriously. He wanted to get ahead. He wanted to create a better life for us."

She paused.

"He began saving money about four years before the priest Crowe took over the parish. He opened a special bank account and kept it secret. Worked extra shifts, weekends… Until the day he sat me down at the kitchen table and showed me the balance statement. He had $17,000 that he had managed to save. *'Louise,'* he told me. *'We're going to be able to open that sporting goods store. Just another year or so and we'll have enough.'* I was very excited. We all were. Not long afterwards…" She flicked a hand at Crowe. "He came."

Calvin Leonard turned to Crowe and rolled a hand,

inviting him to speak.

"I took over at St. Michael and St. Joan's in 1985," he said. "My superior was Archbishop Radcliffe, who you see here beside me. I…was the one who introduced Gordon and Louise to the archbishop during a church social. This would have been around 1986 or so." He cleared his throat. "I noticed they talked, Gordon and the archbishop, for quite a long time. I suppose that was when he broached the topic of Shady Acres with Gordon. The cabins hadn't yet been built but the project was being planned. Arnold McLellan and a few other principals were looking for investors. The archbishop wanted to invest. He had some money put by…"

"And soon he had our money, too!" snapped Louise angrily. She immediately restrained herself. "I'm sorry, Calvin. But…it's painful to remember."

As Barrett watched, the Chief rose and went to stand behind her. He placed a hand on her shoulder. And that was enough.

Crowe sighed. "Let's cut to the chase, here. The archbishop convinced Gordon to give him his savings, presumably on the premise that he could double his money. These he combined with his own savings by way of a seed investment. The cabins were built. And, for a time, the community showed a profit." He produced some pages and handed them across to Calvin. "It's all there. The bank records for the transactions. And the correspondence I wrote, covering for the archbishop. As you can see, he made a tidy profit."

"One hundred and twenty-four thousand dollars," said Calvin quietly, examining the sheets.

"He still has the money," Crowe said. "It represents his life savings. He was planning to use it to go into assisted living. But, under the circumstances…"

"You're going to pay us back what Gordon gave him?" Louise asked.

"No."

A moment of shocked silence rocked the circle until Crowe spoke again.

"We're going to give you the entire sum. By way of reconciliation." He turned to Radcliffe. "I will pay for the archbishop's assisted living costs out of pocket myself."

For the first time since he had met her, Barrett saw Louise Joe's expression soften.

"I'm very sorry," Crowe said finally. "I apologize on behalf of myself, the archbishop, and the Catholic Church. We beg your forgiveness. And Danny…" He turned to the ordained. "I hope you will return to us."

Danny nodded. Louise and Connie smiled.

"Thank you, Archbishop Crowe," said the Chief softly.

"As long as I'm parish priest here," Barrett said, "I promise you. Nothing like this will *ever* happen again. And I hope…you all might consider coming back to church someday."

Louise Joe, Calvin Leonard, and the Chief shared a look. They seemed to accept Barrett's words in the spirit they were intended.

"I guess we're done here," Calvin Leonard said quietly. "Archbishop Crowe? You'll be heading back to Vancouver tonight?"

"We will." He patted Radcliffe's knee. "Got to get this one settled in his new assisted living facility. Looking forward to it, your excellency?"

"Ha!"

Barrett suppressed a smile.

Happily Ever

"HEY."

"Hey."

She stepped into the kitchen and they wrapped their arms around each other. Barrett closed his eyes and took in the sensation of her—scent, strength, and the rough fabric of her tweed jacket. It felt so good to hold her. They remained together like that for a long time.

"So!" With a squeeze she let him go and stepped back. Kicking off her sneakers, she asked: "How about a drink?"

"Done."

He marched over to the sink, grappled down the boxed wine from the cabinet above the basin and turned to find her staring at him with a species of amused horror.

"Boxed wine?" She shook her head. "I treat you to an aged Bordeaux and you return the favor with vino shrink-wrapped in plastic?"

"It still does the trick."

"Barbarian!"

"Here." He poured her a glass and pressed it into her hands. "Drink."

She waited for him to fill his mug before raising her wine. "A toast? How about to Louise Joe and her family? To a successful act of reconciliation?"

He smiled. "To justice served," he said quietly.

They clinked vessels and drank.

"So, what's for dinner?" she asked. "I'm starved."

"Have a seat." Barrett pulled out a chair from the kitchen table. "Watch while I make magic."

"Ho *ho*. This ought to be good," she said, sliding into a chair.

Barrett set to work. He wasn't spectacularly talented in the kitchen, but there were a few dishes he could make reasonably well. Despite his bandaged wrist, he managed to move with his usual dexterity. He switched on the stove, getting the element busy heating up the potato wedges already in place in the oven. Dipping into the fridge, he produced an egg carton, butter and cream. He set four eggs to poach, put two English muffins in the toaster and began making Hollandaise sauce.

"Good lord, Barrett. Are you whipping up eggs bennie?"

"One of my favorites," he chuckled.

"Mine, too!" She finished her wine, padded over to the box on the counter and sluiced another serving from the spigot into her glass. "Man, you got good taste. In food. Wine." She paused, then raised her glass and added: "Women."

Barrett turned and gazed into her eyes. They remained like that for a long time.

"Your eggs are starting to boil over," she whispered romantically.

Barrett laughed and got back to work. Once the

sauce had thickened sufficiently, he laid ham on the freshly-toasted English muffins and began spooning out the eggs. The phone rang as he was finishing up. He checked the caller ID. It was Gavin Lewis.

"Sorry," he said. "I've got to take this."

"Anything I can do?"

"Keep an eye on the wedges, will you?"

"Roger that."

Barrett walked into the living room and answered the call. "Hey, Gavin. Just making dinner. How're you?"

"Oh fine, padre. I won't keep you." Barrett heard papers rustling in the background. "I have to get up to the hospital soon, anyway. Walton's being released and I've agreed to drive him home."

"Please give him our best."

"Will do… Eh, *our* best?"

"Uh, Reverend Ward is here."

"Nice! Like I said. You two make a cute couple." Gavin laughed. "Just wanted to check and see how the reconciliation meeting went."

"Very well. Full restitution to Louise Joe. With interest. And an apology from all of us. Also, we found Danny."

"That's good news." Gavin sounded relieved. "In the midst of everything else. That young man is going to do a lot of good for this town."

"I hope so. How're the loose ends of the investigation coming?"

"Good. Actually, that's why I called." Gavin paused. "We found the Messiah's body down in the junk yard at the bottom of the hill. He'd been shot in a grotesque and brutal manner. Bullets through the knees, ankles, wrists…"

"That's…unfortunate."

"Yeah, well… He was shot with my gun, padre. Ballistics confirmed it. I know you and Reverend Ward raided my gun cabinet for your rescue mission. Just wanted to ask… You wouldn't happen to know anything about—"

"No."

There was a long pause.

"That's sort of what I figured." He sighed. "The gun was found a short distance off. No prints on it."

"I lost it sometime during the firefight."

"I see. Well. I suppose it's possible one of his minions might have gotten ahold of it and…"

"That sounds most likely."

"Most likely. Sure." Gavin coughed. "Well, all things being equal, we don't plan to dig into it too deeply."

"Probably a good idea."

"Yeah." Gavin sighed again. "I'll let you get back to dinner."

"Cheers."

Barrett hung up and returned to the kitchen. Kelly was stirring the Hollandaise sauce.

"I rescued the wedges from the oven," she said, pointing. "And I ate one."

"Did you, now?" Barrett plucked two from the tray, popped one into his mouth and went to her, holding the second up. "Open wide," he teased.

She did and he fed her the wedge. She took it delicately, like a bird, but did not let his fingers get away. She kissed them, drew him to her and found his lips with her own.

It was a long, slow, sensual kiss.

———

AFTERWARDS, they sat together over the ruins of their dinner. They went light on the wine, preferring to be intoxicated by one another's presence, their mutual affection embodied in light 'mistaken' touches of hands, knees, and feet below the table. After a time, they held hands. Kelly's thumb ran back and forth across the back of his knuckles.

"I'm falling in love with you, Mike," she said quietly.

"I…" Some hard, tight place in his chest unknotted and his eyes moistened. "I…love…"

"Shh." Seeing how hard it was for him, she squeezed his hand and leaned forward. "I know, Mike. It's okay."

"I love you, too," he managed to whisper finally.

They moved into each other's arms. Their caresses were more urgent now. As he grappled her to him, Barrett allowed his hand to stray down her back to her ass. He cupped it. Pulled her into him. Moaned into the flexing pulse that was their joined mouths.

"Bedroom," she whispered when the kiss ended. "I want you inside me."

Their trip down the hall was interrupted by several stops to touch and undress each other. By the time they reached the bed, they both had on only pants. They fell across the mattress, entwined in each other…

Their lovemaking was passionate, athletic and infinitely tender.

HE AWOKE AT 2 AM, got cigarettes and sat in a chair beside the bed, watching her sleep.

He would awaken her in another few hours and drive her home before Miss Dolan arrived for the day's work.

Then he would return and try to figure out what to do about his broken vows.

I can't believe I'm doing this, he thought.

But...he loved her. And after a lifetime of trauma, violence, isolation, and betrayal, that was something worth treasuring. A pearl of great price.

I love her, he thought again.

He sat there smoking in the darkness for a long time, trying to decide what he was going to do about it.

If you like this, you may also
enjoy: Old Habits
BY RYAN FOWLER

Tag Nolan was a legend in the Houston, Texas Police Department. Along with his wife, Jenna, he was one of the best detectives H-Town had to offer. But after being shot in the line of duty, he decided on a drastic career change.

Now rector at St. Joseph's Episcopal Church, Father Nolan still serves and protects. Just in a different way.

Unable to set aside a strange encounter with a parishioner and his teen daughter, he and Jenna decide to pay Sean and Annie Holleran a visit…but they're too late. Sean has been beaten bloody—and Annie is missing.

With police targeting the teenage girl as the case's prime suspect, Father Nolan's instincts tell him a different story— Annie is in trouble.

Immersed knee-deep in a twisted and ever-evolving mystery involving gang members, corrupt FBI agents, and stolen drug money, a dedicated Anglican priest and his headstrong wife must confront imminent danger around every corner as they fight to return a young girl home.

AVAILABLE NOVEMBER 2022

About the Author

Jamie Mason is the author of several science fiction novels and thrillers. Born in Montreal, he attended the University of Arizona and Chapman University. After a decade spent teaching in the southwest, he returned to Canada in 2005. He has worked variously as a think-tank analyst, a business manager, a professional musician and a private investigator. Now semi-retired and living in the woods of Vancouver Island, he devotes his time to writing and savoring the vanishing Canadian wilderness.

www.ingramcontent.com/pod-product-compliance
Lightning Source LLC
Chambersburg PA
CBHW010820250626
47156CB00011B/3137